5-

$\frac{10}{19}$

The Talented Mr. Ripley

The Talented Mr. Ripley

A SCREENPLAY BY

Anthony Minghella

Based on the Novel by Patricia Highsmith

**talk
miramax
books**

HYPERION

NEW YORK

LIBRARY OF CONGRESS CATALOGING-IN-PUBLICATION DATA
0-7868-8521-1

FIRST EDITION

10 9 8 7 6 5 4 3 2 1

Acknowledgments

Bill Horberg and Tom Sternberg have been custodians of this project for longer than I have and I must thank them both for inviting me into the strange world of Tom Ripley. They have been passionate and patient supporters on the long journey this screenplay has taken to reach its present form. They join a list of regular and inspiring accomplices, who include John Seale, Paul Zaentz, Ann Roth, Gary Jones, Gabriel Yared, Lynn Kamern, Ivan Sharrock, David Rubin, Leslee Dart, Larry Kaplan, Phil Bray, Pat Jackson, Dennis Lowe, Deborah Ross, Bob Randles, Emma Schofield, Steve Andrews, my partner-in-crime, and Carolyn Choa, my partner-in-life. A glance at the end credits should be enough to dispel any notion that filmmaking is an auteur activity, even when the director is also the film's writer; and I am in debt to every one of the names listed there.

Sydney Pollack has been a quiet, generous guide—a teacher disguising himself as a peer. What a luxury to have a mentor and friend as producer. For a second time, but not—I hope—for the last,

Walter Murch has lent his big brain to me, first during the various drafts of the screenplay, then in the laboratory of his cutting room. This version of the screenplay reflects the discoveries and elisions we made there. There is nobody more rigorous or devoted than Walter and he has made me a better writer and a better director. Roy Walker's production design wisdom encouraged me to amend the more foolish of my schemes and reshape the material—sometimes to fit what we found, sometimes to visually intensify what I had imagined. Once again, Diane Dreyer, the script supervisor, cajoled me to improve the screenplay while filming and Mark Levinson, the ADR supervisor, with equal tenacity, required me to improve the screenplay after filming. Special thanks to them both and their contribution; their names roll by on the film without the recognition they deserve.

Michael Peretzian and Judy Daish have been loyal enthusiasts longer than we care to remember, and I thank them again, as I do the kitchen cabinet of Maura Dooley, Michael Ondaatje, Barry Hirsch, Cassius Matthias, Duncan Kenworthy, Geoff Stier, and my brother, Dominic Minghella, who have cast their kind but critical eyes over successive drafts. Tim Bricknell has been my most faithful ally and truthteller on every day of this project.

My writing has profited, as always, from a terrific cast. In particular, Matt Damon, keeping his pen resolutely in his pocket, has been the best partner in realising this film that any writer could wish for. He has cared for this screenplay as if it were his own, teasing out every nuance, investing his energy and mind and, most significantly, his talent. Alessandro Fabrizi, who translated the screenplay and who helped me in my work with the Italian cast, is one of many colleagues who make shooting a movie in Italy such a pleasure. Being there it's hard to see the point of being anywhere else. I relocated the period of the movie to coincide with what was known as Il Boom, the time in which Italy emerged from the damage and doldrums of the war, and I took much vicarious pleasure, as we pulled locations into the look and feel of the late fifties, from imagining that *La Dolce*

Vita was being filmed around the corner from us. Sandy Von Normann organised that movie as well as *Ripley*, and his personal memory of the times, his loving spirit and his indomitable energy are imprinted on every frame of the film. He told me that in Italy they say, "Never twice but three times," and I count on that being true. *Nel cuore sono italiano.*

Finally, my family has put up with another interminable absence with the same unwarranted good grace. Making films for me is like travelling into a long tunnel. And how lucky I am to have them waiting in the light.

Anthony Minghella
Berkeley, September 1999

Introduction

For children are innocent and love justice; while most of us are wicked and naturally prefer mercy.

C. K. CHESTERTON

Just after I graduated from University I was commissioned to write a small play for the local theatre company. The opportunity came on the back of a fledgling excursion into writing when, as a student, I had sufficient hubris to present a musical, which I also directed, acted and sang in. I cringe at the thought of it. Nevertheless, the playwright Alan Plater, then chairman of the theatre company, saw enough in my crude efforts to give me the chance to work with professional actors. I duly wrote the play, now long discarded, and directed it. My chief memory of the experience was at an early performance on tour in Grimsby, where our audience comprised mainly coach parties shipped in from homes for the elderly. The play began with a lengthy and bleak monologue in the dark. I thought of it as extremely dramatic. After a few minutes the audience felt moved to complain noisily of what they assumed was an electrical failure. Then they proceeded to head for the exit. Alan's programme notes described the play as being in the spirit of Patricia Highsmith. I had never heard of Patricia Highsmith, but thought I should go and find some of her work. The book I stumbled across concerned the exploits of a young American living in Europe called Tom Ripley.

Almost twenty years later, Sydney Pollack, another mentor, asked me to adapt *The Talented Mr. Ripley* for his company. At that time I was marooned in my attempts to make *The English Patient* and felt—on the basis of my one, specious and not entirely auspicious connection to the author—that it might be something to consider.

In the Ripley novels, of which *The Talented Mr. Ripley* is the first, a person can live or die, sometimes literally, on the strength of their choice of cocktail. Taste is everything. Highsmith rarely describes the physical geography, eschews adjectives, sketches out a moment in impatient and irritable prose. There seems little distance between her own baleful view of the world and that of her protagonist's, who travels through a handful of novels, behaving badly, never caught.

You enter into an airless, claustrophobic world with Tom Ripley. Almost no other character is fully alive, and his cool, dislocated perspective lures the reader in, convincing us that what objectively might be heinous makes perfect sense inside Ripley's head. The world, experienced through this skinless sensibility, is an alarming place—Ripley *feels* so intensely, can be giddy with excitement or despair, can plummet into the abyss, is always an outsider, straining for companionship but destined to be alone. His actions are an extreme response to emotions all of us recognise: the sense that there is a better life being lived by somebody else, somewhere else, someone not trapped inside the hollow existence in which we find ourselves. It's one of the things which makes us human. At some time or another we've all been Tom Ripley, just as we've all known a Dickie Greenleaf, the man who has everything, whose attention makes us feel special and important. We've all basked in the sunshine of that attention and felt the chill of losing it.

It was this unsettling connection to Ripley, one of the most fascinatingly flawed characters in fiction, and the anxiety that what happens to him is familiar, at least in nightmares, that prompted me to make this film. Not the empathy for a hero, but the queasy recognition that this plausible misfit is not so far from one version of ourselves; not approval but an acknowledgment that this is where we might end up without the reassuringly tight belt of morality cinched around our waists. In adapting the novel to film lay the challenge of exciting the audience to commit to the material as I did as a reader: to inhabit each step of Ripley's journey until, like a child in the sea who has forgotten the tide, we look back and see how perilously far we are from the shore.

Adaptation for film is, by definition, a process of editorialising. The dramatist is obliged to make innumerable decisions: what is the book about? How will it fit into the proscribed length of a movie, how to dramatise the secret thoughts and aspirations the novelist can describe but the film can only suggest; where to begin; how to end; how to collect the tone of the prose? The answers to these questions must inevitably speak as loudly about the preoccupations of the filmmaker as they do the contingent issues of phrasing the material and organising the story for a film audience to enjoy and follow. Part of the business of reading is to create an inner cinema on which the events play out. And we can be sure that for each reader the film is different. Adaptation is, finally, sharing one inner cinema with an audience. *This is how it felt to me, this is what I thought I was reading.* The dramatist becomes an enthusiastic messenger, bringing news from somewhere else, remembering the best bits, exaggerating the beauty, relishing the mystery, probing the moral imperative, watching for gasps or tears, orchestrating them and, ideally, prompting the captive cinema audience to make the pilgrimage back to the book, which remains blessedly itself. But as Italo Calvino said of storytelling, the tale is not beautiful if nothing is added to it. The demands of film are also a release, enabling the writer to emphasise and mute by turns. The screenplay, obliged to work in its own right, is both an argument with the source material and a commentary on it. The uninflected brilliance of Highsmith's novel, its disavowal of moral consequence, Ripley's solipsism, the author's acerbic judgment of everybody other than Ripley, the book's heavy employment of devices—letters, coincidences—do not sit easily within the context of film.

But if the intimate gestures of a novel, its private conversation between writer and reader, are not available to the filmmaker, they are exchanged for other, equally powerful, tools. Film grammar, with its unique ability to manipulate images, flexing from the intense close-up to the broadest vistas, is perfectly placed to situate personal behaviour in a public landscape. It can contextualise action, remind us that how we are as individuals is in thrall quite literally to the bigger picture.

> *This was the clean slate he had thought about on the boat crossing over from America. This was the real annihilation of his past and himself, Tom Ripley, who was made up of that past, and his rebirth as a completely new person.*[1]

My reading of Ripley's isolation at the end of the novel, however much he fantasises about the freedom his lies and improvisations have earned him, is that it contains an implicit cautionary tale. What the reader knows is that Ripley's clean slate is an illusion, one which the game of travel encourages. The rebirth is a temporary disguise and, worse, one that condemns the impostor to a constant fear of exposure and the humiliation which follows. To be uncovered as a sham is the very thing which prompts Ripley to sham in the first place. And so the film came to hinge on a central premise: Ripley's credo that it is better to be a fake somebody than a real nobody. It becomes a story about class.

The novel is about a man who commits murders and is not caught. And so the film is about a man who commits murders and is not caught. But it departs in one crucial sense by concluding that eluding public accountability is not the same thing as eluding justice. The film has a moral imperative: You can get away with murder, but you don't really get away with anything. Ripley, always looking for love, always looking to love and be loved, has to kill his opportunity for love. He ends the movie alone, free, and in a hell of his own making. Just as in Dante, where purgatory is some karmic reflection of life—flatterers pitched in manure, adulterers chasing forever—so in annihilating self, assuming someone's identity, Ripley is condemned never to be free to be truly himself ever again.

This tragic dimension provided an architecture for the screenplay. Its ambitions were to maintain the narrative ambivalence of the novel—not telling an audience what to think, not opting for an announced moral closure, but intensifying the consequence of Ripley's actions on the soul. Without the reassuring appearance of a judge, the audience is asked to be a jury. A number of choices stem directly from this strategy. A signal adjustment to the novel is that Ripley does not plan to kill Dickie; quite the reverse. The death scene begins with Ripley's revealing the depth of his feelings for Dickie, horribly miscalculated, cruelly rejected. Dickie dies in an eruption of rage and it is his own capacity for violence which exacerbates a reflexive swing of an oar into a do-or-die struggle. It's an accident which inadvertently provides Ripley with a defining opportunity. And, as so often in this story, it's an opportunity he seizes as much in shame as in calculation. Ripley's journey to purgatory begins with the borrowing of a jacket, because he doesn't possess a decent one of his own. It continues, for what he feels are the same reasons, with the borrowing of an identity.

Peter Smith-Kingsley, mentioned only in passing in the novel, becomes a fully-fledged character in the film. His acceptance of Ripley as Ripley suggested itself as a required irony, a way of dramatising what Highsmith called the annihilation of Ripley's past and himself; in killing Peter he murders his own chance of happiness. Peter, the most centered character in the film, also serves as a reminder that Ripley's pathology is not explained by his sexuality. Similarly, Herbert Greenleaf's relationship with Dickie developed into a crucial strand. The film's mechanism of lies and escape depends on a father's lack of faith in his son, a prejudgment that makes him incapable of seeing Ripley's hand in what has happened. In this way Ripley can appear to be the better version of Dickie, the son Herbert Greenleaf wishes he had. No one in this story sees truth in front of them because of the distortions of their own particular prejudices and preconceptions. Only Marge Sherwood, in a more substantive role than the novel allows, has a sufficiently uncluttered spirit to both welcome Ripley and then suspect him. But the collusion of men, which is such a feature of this story and of the times, undermines her. They are too busy covering up, preferring to interpret Marge's unerring radar for the truth as the misguided forensics of heartbreak. Meredith Logue, a new character for the film, gives Ripley the chance to create his own version of Marge, just as he creates his own version of Dickie. Her presence also accentuates that this is principally a story about young people, each of whom has run away from something, making themselves up in the context of a foreign country, *partners*, as Meredith observes giddily, *in disguise.*

That foreign country is Italy.

> *Rome was chic. Rome was part of his new life. He wanted to be able to say in Majorca or Athens or Cairo or wherever he was: "Yes, I live in Rome. I keep an apartment there."*

For two generations before Ripley, Americans had been coming to Europe to explore issues of identity and sexuality. It's no accident that Patricia Highsmith herself had settled in Europe in the 1950s and would have been a contemporary of Marge and Meredith. Nor is it an accident that her book is loosely based on *The Ambassadors*, the work of an earlier and more celebrated expatriate, Henry James. The idea of the Grand Tour, of exploring the Old Country, of soaking in the culture of Europe, continues to exert an irresistible tug on American travellers long after Europe's culture has been conquered and transformed by America. Italy, a substantial character in this film, its landscape largely intact from the Renaissance paintings which celebrate it, its history as the artistic and classical heart of the continent, has particular appeal.

Was it, in short, ever well to be elsewhere when one might be in Italy? wrote Edith Wharton. By locating the movie a year or two later than the novel, there was an opportunity to explore a significant moment in Italian history, where a thin veneer of the modern, the sophistication of La Dolce Vita, had glossed but could not entirely hide the more primitive mores of the country. Italy is a place I love above all other places, but it's always possible to detect a darker note sounding under its breezy melodies. And this dissonance seemed to speak of the film itself, apparently sybaritic, but lounging on a volcano. Mongibello, the name Highsmith gave to the fictional village on the Amalfi coast where Dickie and Marge are living, is a local name for Vesuvius.

Finally, a film called *The Talented Mr. Ripley* had to address Ripley's talents. If Ripley is blessed and cursed by one thing, it is his ability to turn on a dime, to reel off the most elaborate and plausible riffs of fantasy. In identifying this, the importance of music grew in my mind, replacing the more literary motif of painting in the novel. Music for period, music for place, music for argument. And so the screenplay also became a kind of libretto, working out relationships in musical terms, pitting Dickie's identification with jazz, its mantra of freedom and existentialism, against Ripley's formal classicism and asserting that, just as in music, where truly great extemporising begins with Bach and Mozart, so it is Ripley who proves to be the more genuine improviser.

When I adapted *The English Patient* I was accompanied on an adventure that involved wholesale reimagining of that magnificent novel by Michael Ondaatje himself, holding up a compass, endorsing every act of omission and commission, encouraging my most extravagant inventions. Patricia Highsmith died as I began writing the first draft of *Ripley* and before I could meet her. If I were to have pleased anybody with this adaptation I would have liked it to have been her and I worked with her own pungent words about fiction as a touchstone. She imagined Ripley sitting at the typewriter with her as she wrote her novel. I imagined her sitting with me as I wrote my screenplay.

> *If a suspense writer is going to write about murderers and victims, about people in the vortex of this awful whirl of events, he must do more than describe brutality and gore. He should be interested in justice or the absence of it in the world, good and bad, and in human cowardice or courage—but not merely as forces to move his plot in one direction. In a word his invented people must seem real.[2]*

Anthony Minghella
Berkeley, September 1999

1. *The Talented Mr. Ripley*, Patricia Highsmith
2. *Plotting and Writing Suspense Fiction*, Patricia Highsmith

Author's Note

This screenplay represents a snapshot of the film at the end of
October 1999. The editing process continues and will, inevitably,
result in changes, minor or substantial, from what is published here.

AM

PROLOGUE: INT. RIPLEY'S CABIN. EVENING.

Fade up on Ripley, as in the final scene of the film, sitting, desolate in a ship's cabin. The camera rotates around his face, which begins in light and ends in darkness.

> RIPLEY (O/S)
> If I could just go back. If I could rub everything out. Starting with myself. Starting with borrowing a jacket.

1958

—

A vinyl RECORD revolves in close-up.

An exuberant and mysterious VOICE is scat singing. Wild. Then the sound slides into a raucous big band jazz number: Dizzy Gillespie's *The Champ*. CREDITS begin.

INT. RIPLEY'S APARTMENT, NEW YORK. DAY.

A HAND ejects the record. When the camera finds the man's face it is **BLINDFOLDED**. He's hot. He's wearing an undershirt. He's trying to identify the recording.

> RIPLEY (O/S)
> I don't know. Count Basie? Duke Ellington. I don't know. Count Basie.

The man pulls off the blindfold, examines the record cover of the disc he's been trying to learn, needs to put on glasses to do so, is irritated by his mistake. He ejects the record.

A pile of other jazz records are strewn across a cluttered table which includes classical sheet music and a paper keyboard.

One hand idly mimes at the keys. **Piano music sounds as if by magic, a clear soprano voice above it.**

EXT. CENTRAL PARK WEST TERRACE. EARLY EVENING.

Ripley is at the piano, accompanying FRAN, a young soprano.

>   **F R A N   (SINGS)**
> *Ah, such fleeting paradise*
> *such innocent delight*
> *to love,*
> *be loved,*
> *a lullabye,*
> *then silence.*

The song finishes. Applause. They're the entertainment at a cocktail party to celebrate a silver wedding anniversary. Some partygoers congratulate Fran on her performance. A distinguished-looking man, pushing his wife in a wheelchair, approaches Ripley, offers his hand.

>   **HERBERT GREENLEAF**
> Most enjoyable. Herbert Greenleaf.

>   **RIPLEY**
> Tom Ripley. Thank you, sir.

>   **HERBERT GREENLEAF**
>   *(pointing at Ripley's borrowed jacket)*
> I see you were at Princeton.
> Then you'll most likely know our son, Dick.
> Dickie Greenleaf...

>   **EMILY GREENLEAF**
> We couldn't help noticing your jacket.

>   **RIPLEY**
>   *(hesitating)*
> How is Dickie?

INT. ELEVATOR OPENING OUT INTO LOBBY. EARLY EVENING.

Fran, Ripley, Mr. and Mrs. Greenleaf and others emerge from an elevator. Emily talks to Fran, Herbert to Ripley.

> EMILY GREENLEAF
> *(to Fran)*
> I hope you'll come and see us...

> FRAN
> That's very kind.

> EMILY GREENLEAF
> Both of you...

> HERBERT GREENLEAF
> Of course, Dickie's idea of music is jazz. He
> has a saxophone. To my ear jazz is just
> noise, just an insolent noise.

INT. RIPLEY'S APARTMENT. CONTINUOUS FROM FIRST SCENE.

Another song for Ripley to identify is on the gramophone. Chet Baker's *My Funny Valentine*. Signs everywhere of packing. A suitcase. Books about Italy. Ripley paces in this **BASEMENT** room, which is bathroom, kitchen, living room and bedroom all in one. Tiny, tidy, squalid and sad. The windows give onto bars and a wall.

> RIPLEY
> Don't even know if this is a man or a woman.

There's a violent row going on in the room above his head. He flinches.

EXT. CENTRAL PARK WEST. EARLY EVENING.

Ripley shakes hands with Herbert Greenleaf as he gets into his Rolls-Royce. They are making an appointment. Ripley

crosses the street to Fran, pecks her cheek. She hands him
his share of their fee.

RIPLEY

Gotta run. I'm so late.
(he hands Fran's boyfriend the jacket he's been wearing)
Thanks for the jacket.

BOYFRIEND

Sure. Thanks for filling in for me.

From Greenleaf's point of view he sees a couple embracing.

EMILY GREENLEAF

Darling couple aren't they?

HERBERT GREENLEAF

Yes. An exceptional young man.

From another vantage point Ripley hurries on as Fran gets
into her boyfriend's car. A piano quartet starts up.

EXT. THEATER. EVENING.

Ripley runs past the droves of arriving concertgoers and
heads for the theater. Music continues.

INT. MEN'S ROOM, THEATER. NIGHT.

The interval: A thick mass of men in tuxedoes grooming
themselves at the basins. Ripley turns on faucets, offers towels, brushes off dandruff. Men talk over, round and through
him. Put coins in a bowl.

INT. A BOX AT THE THEATER. NIGHT.

The concert continues. Ripley peers through the curtain at
the performances. A haughty woman in the box turns round
and he closes the curtain.

INT. BACKSTAGE. 1:30 A.M.

An empty auditorium. Ripley plays Bach in the blue ghost-light. A caretaker emerges from his rounds, flips on the houselights. Ripley jerks up from his playing, waves apologetically.

>   RIPLEY
>   Sorry, sorry. I know. Sorry.

INT. RIPLEY'S APARTMENT. DAY.

Ripley, shining his shoes, packing almost done, is testing himself on another piece of music. Free jazz saxophone: Charlie Parker's *Koko*. He listens hard, recognizes the track.

>   RIPLEY
>   That's Charlie Parker. Bird.

He skips over to the gramophone, checks the record. He's right, he smiles.

EXT. GREENLEAF SHIPYARDS, BROOKLYN. DAY.

Greenleaf and Ripley walk through one of the drydocks. A huge void in the shape of a boat, swarming with workers preparing the shell of a new liner. If Central Park is where the money is spent, this is clearly where it's made. And a lot of it. Workers nod deferentially to the man with his name over the buildings behind them.

>   HERBERT GREENLEAF
>   Mongibello. Tiny place. South of Naples.
>   Marge, his, uh, the young lady is supposedly
>   writing some kind of book. God knows what
>   he does. By all accounts they spend the
>   whole time on the beach. Or his sailboat.
>   That's my son's talent, spending his
>   allowance.

Ripley, in his green corduroy jacket the very model of a sober young man, listens attentively.

                    HERBERT GREENLEAF

Could you ever conceive of going to Italy,
Tom, persuade my son to come home?
                    (Ripley looks doubtful)
I'd pay you. I'd pay you one thousand
dollars.

                    RIPLEY

I've always wanted to go to Europe, sir,
but...

                    HERBERT GREENLEAF

Good. Now you can go for a reason.

Greenleaf walks off towards his waiting limousine.

INT. RIPLEY'S APARTMENT. DAY.

Ripley studies an old photograph of Dickie Greenleaf in a
Princeton yearbook. He shoves the book in a bag, picks up
his suitcase and takes a last look around the dingy apartment
before closing the door beind him.

EXT. RIPLEY'S APARTMENT. DAY.

Ripley hauls his luggage up the stairs and into the sunlight.
He is met at the top of the stairs by Mr. Greenleaf's
chauffeur.

                    CHAUFFEUR

Here. I'll take that.

                    RIPLEY

Thanks.

                    CHAUFFEUR
                (nodding towards the apartment)
That thousand bucks should come in handy.

                    RIPLEY

Yes, sir.

CHAUFFEUR
(interrupts Ripley, who is about to open the car door)
I'll get that.

RIPLEY
Thanks.

CHAUFFEUR
(as he holds open the door for Ripley)
Sir.
(Ripley laughs excitedly)
You're gonna have a great trip. Mr. Greenleaf
is personal friends with the Cunard people.

INT. HERBERT GREENLEAF'S CAR. DAY.

Ripley luxuriates in the back of the Greenleaf limousine. He opens up an envelope he's carrying with Greenleaf stationery. Inside a first-class Cunard ticket, some traveler's checks and dollars.

CHAUFFEUR
I can tell you. The Greenleaf name opens a
lot of doors.

EXT. *QUEEN MARY*. MANHATTAN SKYLINE.
DAY.

The liner leaves New York en route to Italy. END CREDITS.

INT. NAPLES HARBOR, CUSTOMS & IMMIGRA-
TION HALL. DAY.

Italy. Brilliant sunshine. The *Queen Mary* has just docked. Passengers can be seen disembarking through the huge windows. Coming from the first-class gangways, they are greeted, escorted, fussed over into the hall. Their bags have been unloaded ahead of them, and are now being sorted in the hall under the initials of their owners. Stands with the letters of the alphabet chalked on them are dotted about, and trunks and suitcases of all shapes and sizes form small hills around them. Ripley enters and an Italian porter approaches, wants his name. *Ripley. Ripley. Ripley.* He repeats in the hubbub and joins the crowd around the letter **R.** A striking young woman (MEREDITH) is nearby. She notices him.

Ripley proceeds to the Customs area, where he's held in a line as a large suitcase is opened and searched. Meredith catches up with him. Her luggage a mountain next to his.

> MEREDITH
>
> What's your secret?

> RIPLEY
>
> Excuse me?

> MEREDITH
>
> No, it's just—you are American, aren't you?
> —no, I just, I have so much luggage, and
> you're so, uh, streamlined. It's humiliating.

Ripley shrugs. Now they're opening a second case of the passenger ahead. Hard not to converse.

> MEREDITH
>
> I'm Meredith, by the way. Meredith Randall.

> RIPLEY
>
> Dickie, Dickie Greenleaf. Hello.

> MEREDITH
>
> Hello.

They are passed through Immigration, head down the long stairs towards the street. Meredith catches up with Ripley.

> MEREDITH (CONT'D)
>
> You're not the Shipping Greenleafs?

> RIPLEY
> *(thinking quickly)*
>
> Trying not to be. Trying to jump ship.

MEREDITH

So now did they put your suitcase in the wrong pile?

RIPLEY

Gosh, I didn't know my luggage would be so interesting.

MEREDITH

No, just—upstairs—weren't you under the **R** stand? I thought I saw you there.

RIPLEY

My father wants me in New York. He builds boats. I'd rather sail them. I travel under my mother's name.

MEREDITH

Which is?

RIPLEY

Emily.
                (Meredith's bewildered)
Just kidding.

MEREDITH

The funny thing is, I'm not Randall either. I'm Logue.

RIPLEY
(nods, recognizing the name)
As in the…?

MEREDITH

As in the Textile Logues. Trying to shrug off the dress. I travel under my mother's name, too.

RIPLEY

Randall.

MEREDITH

Right.

They've arrived at a crossroads on the stairs—graphic signs explain the choices: one way for **Buses, Taxis and Exits,** the other for **Trains: ROMA, VENEZIA, MILANO.** They're going in different directions.

> MEREDITH (CONT'D)
> *(offering her hand)*
> So—partners in disguise.
> *(looks at the signs)*
> 'Bye.

EXT. COASTAL ROAD FROM NAPLES. LATE AFTERNOON.

A BUS rolls along a coastal road cut into the side of a cliff, mountain above, blue sea below.

INT. BUS. LATE AFTERNOON.

Ripley sits surrounded by teeming life. The bus slows at a new town. People get off.

INT./EXT. BUS ARRIVES MONGIBELLO. LATE DAY.

Later, the day ending. Ripley looks out as they continue on their journey. Arriving at a small fishing port they wind down through a square, passing the local church.

EXT. MONGIBELLO, FISHERMAN'S WHARF. LATE DAY.

And then the bus is in the heart of a wharf. On one side there's evidence of the fisherman's life, nets, old men working. Opposite there's a tiny café spilling out onto the street, young guys hang out, play table football, lounge on their Vespas. The Driver chants—

> DRIVER
> MONGIBELLO!

Ripley gets out, lugging his cases, as the bus continues on its way. He looks around him. He feels completely foreign.

EXT. MIRAMARE HOTEL/BOAT AT SEA. MORNING.

A SAILBOAT has slid into his view, now drops anchor, drops the sail. A couple dive off and swim towards shore.

ALL OF THIS IS FROM THE POINT OF VIEW OF RIPLEY, who's watching the events through binoculars from his tiny balcony in the Miramare Hotel. An Italian Vocabulary Book is perched on his knees and during this he continues his study, mouthing the Italian words.

> RIPLEY
> *(looking at a long, lean girl about to dive)*
> *La fidanzata a una faccia.* The fiancée has a
> face. *La fidanzata e Marge.*
> *(her partner, DICKIE GREENLEAF, dives, too. They're brown, beautiful, perfect.)*
> *Questo e la mia faccia....* This is my face.
> *(The golden couple emerge from the sea. Dickie shakes off the water, grins.)*
> *Questa...e la mia faccia. Questa e la faccia di Dickie.*

EXT. MONGIBELLO BEACH. DAY.

Ripley emerges from one of the BEACH CABINS, and stands on the edge of the sand on a wooden walkway. He's wearing A TINY LIME-GREEN BATHING SUIT. He loathes beaches. A couple of boys turn laconically and watch him.

Ripley puts on his shoes and scurries to the sea. He feels ridiculous, his skin alabaster against the brown bodies. Finally, the shame is too great and he pulls off his shoes and dashes to the water, where he luxuriates in the coolness of it before wading out of the sea, and walking straight up to Dickie.

RIPLEY

Dickie Greenleaf?

Dickie squints at Ripley, who holds his shoes, lamely.

DICKIE

Who's that?

RIPLEY

It's Tom. Tom Ripley. We were at Princeton
together.

DICKIE

Okay.
(he sits up)
And did we know each other?

RIPLEY

Well, I knew you, so I suppose you must
have known me.

DICKIE
(to Marge)
Princeton is like a fog, America's like a fog.
(to Ripley)
This is Marge Sherwood. Tom—sorry, what
was it?

RIPLEY

Ripley. Hullo. How do you do.

MARGE

How do you do.

DICKIE

What are you doing in Mongi?

RIPLEY

Nothing. Nothing much. Passing through.

DICKIE
(finds this idea absurd)
Passing through! You're so white. Did you

DICKIE (CONT'D)

ever see a guy so white, Marge? Gray, actually.

RIPLEY

It's just an undercoat.

(Marge laughs)

DICKIE

Say again?

RIPLEY

You know, a primer.

DICKIE

That's funny.

He shares some intimacy with Marge, makes her laugh.
Ripley stands as they wrestle around him. Marge looks up.

MARGE

You should come and have lunch with us,
before you go—Dickie?

DICKIE

Sure. Any time.

MARGE

And be careful in the sun. Your gray's in dan-
ger of turning a little pink.

RIPLEY

Thanks. Well, a coincidence.

EXT. MONGIBELLO. EARLY MORNING.

ANOTHER DAY. Church bells ringing. Dickie, dressed in
shorts, comes bumping up the cobbled path towards the
square on his MOTORSCOOTER. He stops by a steep flight
of steps. RIPLEY, a book in hand, unseen, walking up a hill,
catches all this and, intrigued, watches as a young Italian
beauty, SILVANA, has a spiky, flirtatious exchange with
Dickie, then climbs on the scooter behind him.

DICKIE

I've been looking for you everywhere.

SILVANA

Ah, today you're looking for me. And where
have you been the rest of the week? Pig.
With your American girl? I hate you, you
know?

DICKIE

What?

SILVANA

I hate you.

And RIPLEY watches them as they rattle down the hill
towards the sea.

EXT. MONGIBELLO. LATE MORNING.

LATER and Marge struggles up a hill, loaded with groceries.
Ripley comes the other way, casual, still with his book, but
it's not an accidental meeting. Ripley holds up a hand in
greeting. Marge is confused.

RIPLEY

It's Tom, Marge, Tom Ripley.

MARGE

Right! Of course, how are you! We thought
you'd gone.

RIPLEY

No, still here. Getting settled.

MARGE

You must be invisible. Such a small place.

RIPLEY
(a little laugh)

Well.

(he points at her groceries)

— 14 —

RIPLEY (CONT'D)

Can I carry something?

MARGE
(handing over some bags)

Thanks.
(as they walk)

The other day was Dickie not friendly? He
wasn't very, was he?

RIPLEY

No, he was okay.

MARGE

He's allergic, I think, to home. I think he
hears the accent and panics.

RIPLEY

But not yours.

MARGE

No, he panics with me, too, but that's another *storia*, as they say here.

They've reached the bottom of another steep flight of stairs
leading up to Marge's house.

MARGE

This is me. Thanks.

RIPLEY

See you around.

Marge watches him walk away, feels guilty.

MARGE

Tom, what are you doing for lunch?

EXT. MARGE'S HOUSE. AFTERNOON.

Dickie appears in Marge's garden, the sea behind his head.
Marge is standing at her outside table gathering up some of

the remnants of lunch. Dickie's sheepish, showered, late.

> **DICKIE**
> Sorry, sorry, sorry. I know, I'm late, I'm a
> swine.

> **MARGE**
> Did you forget where I live? It's four o'clock.

> **DICKIE**
> I just woke up. I'm sorry.

> **MARGE**
> You just woke up!

INSIDE, washing dishes in the sink, listening, Ripley reacts, knowing this to be a lie.

> **DICKIE (O/S)**
> Fausto and I—we took the boat out, we were
> fishing, and then it was dawn and we'd
> caught absolutely nothing.

> **MARGE (O/S)**
> Well, we ate everything without you.

> **DICKIE (O/S)**
> We?

> **MARGE (O/S)**
> Yes, Tom Ripley's here.

As Ripley appears with the tray to collect more dishes.

> **DICKIE**
> Who? Oh, Tom, hello, how are you? We
> thought you'd disappeared. We were going
> to send out a search party.

> **RIPLEY**
> No, still here.

MARGE

Tom was telling me about his trip over. Made
me laugh so much I got a nosebleed.

DICKIE

Is that good?

MARGE

Shut up!

Marge flicks him with a napkin. They start to wrestle, exclud-
ing Tom.

RIPLEY

I'm intruding.

DICKIE

Can you mix a martini?

RIPLEY
(hesitant)

Sure.

MARGE
(going inside)

I'll do it. I make a fabulous martini.

DICKIE

Everybody should have one talent.
(to Ripley)

What's yours?

RIPLEY
(without a beat)

Forging signatures. Telling lies.
Impersonating practically anybody.

DICKIE
(enjoying this banter)

That's three. Nobody should have more than
one talent. Okay, do an impression.

RIPLEY

Now? Okay. Wait a minute. Talent—

R I P L E Y **(CONT'D)**
(his voice ages, his face changes)
The only talent my son has is for cashing his
allowance.

D I C K I E
(absolutely thrown)
What? What's this?

R I P L E Y

I like to sail, believe me, I love to sail! Instead
I make boats and other people sail them.

D I C K I E
(incredibly impressed)
Stop! It's too much! You're making all the
hairs on my neck stand up!

R I P L E Y
(relishing it)
Jazz, let's face it, it's just an insolent noise.

D I C K I E
I feel like he's here. Horrible. Like the old
bastard is here right now! That's brilliant!
How do you know him?

R I P L E Y
I met him in New York.

D I C K I E
Marge! You've got to hear this!

M A R G E
(returning with the drinks)
What? What?

D I C K I E
Meet my father, Herbert Richard Greenleaf
First.

R I P L E Y
Pleasure to meet you, Dickie's made a fine
catch. I know Emily thinks so.

                        MARGE

What's going on?

                        DICKIE

Uncanny!

                        MARGE

What's this? I don't get it.

                        RIPLEY

Could you ever conceive of going there, Tom,
and bringing him back?

                        DICKIE

What?

                        RIPLEY

I'd pay you. If you would go to Italy and per-
suade my son to come home. I'd pay you one
thousand dollars.

INT./EXT. MONGIBELLO CHURCH AND SQUARE. DUSK.

A christening is over and now the whole village is pouring
out of church for the *Passeggiata* in Sunday best. Girls arm
in arm parade. Boys arm in arm evaluate. New babies are
compared and fussed over. Old people smoke, talk, shrug.
Dickie is walking with Ripley, seething about his father's
scheming.

                        DICKIE

Do you think he's insane?

                        RIPLEY

Who?

                        DICKIE

My father! To actually hire somebody to
come all the way here to drag me back home
—got to be insane, hasn't he?

SILVANA comes out of church arm in arm with a man, her fiancé, as part of a foursome which includes Dickie's pal FAUSTO. Silvana's eyes flick towards Dickie, otherwise there's no acknowledgment as they all greet each other. Dickie introduces Tom, then they move on.

> **RIPLEY**
>
> No, I think your mother, her illness—that's part of your dad's anxiety…

> **DICKIE**
>
> It's got nothing to do with my mother! She's had leukemia for—! This is what makes me boil about him! HE wants me back!—it's got nothing to do with my mother.

> **RIPLEY**
>
> I don't know, Dickie, I'm just telling you what I—

> **DICKIE**
> *(interrupting)*
>
> I set foot back home and he's got a leg-iron waiting at those shipyards and he can't wait to lock me in it and throw away the key. I'm never going back!

> **RIPLEY**
>
> Okay. I don't blame you. It's beautiful here, why would anyone ever want to leave?

EXT. MONGIBELLO BEACH. MORNING.

ANOTHER DAY, Ripley watches from the beach as Dickie's SAILBOAT edges slowly towards the shore. He squints to read the name of the boat—**BIRD**. Fausto, Dickie's friend, goes running off the little jetty and dives into the sea, striking out towards the boat, where Marge puts out the ladder for him to climb in. Then they're off—Dickie skillfully maneuvers the boat into the open sea, the others an obedient crew. Ripley has a tote bag and is working on the stitching. He uses his teeth to TUG at the thread, UNPICKING THE SEAM.

EXT. DICKIE'S HOUSE, MONGIBELLO. AFTERNOON.

Ripley appears, with his meagre luggage, at Dickie's front door. He's carrying the tote bag, stuffed, under his arm. Dickie opens the door.

> RIPLEY
>
> I hope you don't mind. I thought I'd say good-bye. I'm taking off.

> DICKIE
>
> Okay.

Marge has appeared up on the terrace. Dickie looks up.

> DICKIE (CONT'D)
>
> Ripley's saying good-bye.

> MARGE
>
> I'll come down.

> DICKIE
>
> Did you speak to my father?

> RIPLEY
>
> You were right about the telephones. There are no lines, there's some problem.

> MARGE
>
> Hello, Tom. You're off? What are your plans?

> RIPLEY
>
> Back, I suppose, slowly as I can.

He goes to shake her hand and as he releases the tote bag the seam splits and records spill to the ground, scattering. He bends down, starts gathering them up. Marge helps.

R I P L E Y   (CONT'D)

Oh, damn, sorry, this bag's—

Dickie's delighted when he sees the jazz titles.

D I C K I E

You like jazz!

R I P L E Y
(gathering up the records)

I *love* jazz.

D I C K I E
(holding up a Coltrane)

This is the best. Marge says she likes jazz, but she thinks Glenn Miller is jazz.

M A R G E

I've never said that!

R I P L E Y

Bird. That's jazz.

D I C K I E

Bird! Ask me the name of my sailboat—

R I P L E Y

I don't know. What's the name of your sailboat?

D I C K I E

Bird!

M A R G E

Which is ridiculous. Boats are female, everyone knows you can't call a boat after a man.

R I P L E Y

He's not a man, he's a god.

D I C K I E
(excited)

Okay, we're going to Naples. There's a club, it's not a club, it's a cellar.

MARGE

It's vile.

DICKIE

Yes, it's vile. Don't worry, you don't have to
come.
(to Ripley)
It's great. You're going to love it.

INT. JAZZ CLUB, NAPLES. NIGHT.

A cavern blue with smoke. A surprisingly good QUINTET
blast out their version of *MOANIN'*. Dickie and Ripley arrive
and make their way to a table where Fausto is sitting with
friends. It's too noisy for conversation, but Dickie shouts
introductions and they shake Ripley's hand. Dickie is
instantly absorbed in the music, Ripley absorbed in Dickie.
An attractive Italian girl, DAHLIA, comes over, kisses Dickie,
pulls off his hat, puts it on, there's no room for her to sit, so
she sits on Dickie's lap, smoking his cigarette. Dickie raises
his eyebrow at Tom, but it's clearly no hardship. Then the
band strikes up the intro to *Tu vuo' fa' L'Americano*—a hit
which reflects the current craze for all things American—and
Fausto pulls a protesting Dickie up onto the stage.

FAUSTO
(improvising in Italian)
Ladies and Gentlemen. Dickie Greenleaf, all
the way from America... etc.

Fausto starts to sing. Dickie joins in the chorus. Everybody
claps. Dickie talks off-mic to Fausto.

FAUSTO (CONT'D)
And a big round of applause for a new friend
from New York—Tom Ripley!

Ripley's mortified, but Dickie jumps off the stage and pulls
him up. The song continues and now, at the chorus, it's

— 23 —

Dickie and Ripley who have to sing. Ripley, of course, can sing well, if not confidently, in this arena. Soon the audience is clapping, standing on tables, dancing, Dahlia prominent.

> **D I C K I E   (O/S)**
> *(reading)*
> *I have bumped into an old friend from Princeton—a fellow named Tom Ripley. He says he's going to haunt me until I agree to come back to New York with him...*

INT. DICKIE'S HOUSE. NOON.

Dickie, in his new dressing gown, is sitting at the table, typing. Ripley's head emerges from behind the couch on which he has been enjoying a blissful sleep.

> **D I C K I E**
> *(grins)*
> Good afternoon!

> **R I P L E Y**
> Do you always type your letters?
> *(points at the letter)*
> That should be two *T*s.

> **D I C K I E**
> I can't write and I can't spell. That's the privilege of a first-class education. You're upstairs at the back. I think Ermelinda made the bed up.

> **R I P L E Y**
> This is so good of you.

> **D I C K I E**
> Don't say it again. Now you're a Double Agent and we're going to string my dad along, I was thinking we might buy a little car with the expense money he's sending you.

> DICKIE (CONT'D)
>
> What do you think, Marge…a little
> Cinquecento?

Marge has appeared, carrying Camparis.

> MARGE
>
> Dickie, you can't even drive a car! No, what
> we need urgently is an icebox. What do you
> think, Tom? Agree with me and I'll be your
> friend for life.

> RIPLEY
>
> I absolutely agree with Marge.

INT. DICKIE'S HOUSE, UPSTAIRS. DAY.

Ripley locates his room, puts down his luggage in what is a
comfortable and simple room, then heads back downstairs
only to be tempted by the open door of Dickie's bedroom.

INT. DICKIE'S BEDROOM. DAY.

Ripley explores the casual elegance of Dickie's bedroom—
the Louis Vuitton chest, the closet's open door spilling out
shirts, ties. On the dressing table there are toiletries, cuff
links scattered, a silk tie. Ripley picks up the tie and walks
towards the open window below which is a terrace where
lunch is being laid. Marge and Dickie are chatting as Dickie
opens a bottle of wine. Shreds of conversation float up to
Ripley.

> DICKIE
>
> It'll just be for a little while. He can be… he
> makes me laugh.

> MARGE
>
> Okay, darling.

> DICKIE
>
> You'd say if you mind?

MARGE

No, I like him.

DICKIE

Marge, you like everybody.

MARGE

I don't like you.

DICKIE

Then I'll go to your place and you can move
in with Tom.

Above them, Ripley repeats these phrases, carefully, testing
the cadences, *No, I like him. Marge, you like everybody*, until
he's as accurate as a tape recorder.

EXT. TERRACE OF DICKIE'S HOUSE. DAY.

Ermelinda is clearing away lunch. Ripley is changed and sitting at the table with Marge while Dickie works on the coffee.
Ripley watches him, studying everything: the way he uses the
expresso machine, the way he wears no socks, his pants, his
rings.

DICKIE

Now you know why Miss Sherwood always
shows up for breakfast. It's not love, it's the
coffee machine.

MARGE

It's the one task Dickie can do on his
own—make coffee.

DICKIE

Shut up.

MARGE

Oh darling—is that for me?

DICKIE

No, it's for Tom as he didn't complain.

RIPLEY
(as Dickie hands him his cup)

That ring's so great. The green one.

MARGE
(delighted)

Tom, I love you!
(to Dickie)

See!
(to Ripley)

I bought it for him, for his birthday.

RIPLEY

It's superb.

DICKIE

I had to promise, capital P, never to take it off
—otherwise I'd give it to you.

MARGE
(flicking a crumb at him)

Bastard!
(to Ripley)

Isn't it great, Tom? I found it in Naples. I
bargained for about two weeks.

DICKIE

I hope it wasn't cheap.

RIPLEY
(to Marge)

I have to find a birthday present for Frances.
Perhaps you can help me?

MARGE

Frances?

RIPLEY

My fiancée.

DICKIE

You're a dark horse, Ripley. Engaged?

                    RIPLEY

Your parents met her.

                    DICKIE

Oh God—I can just imagine—*if only Dickie
would settle down...doesn't every parent
deserve a grandchild?* Never! I swear on your
ring, Marge. I am never going back.

EXT. *BIRD* SAILBOAT. DAY.

The *Bird* is sailing off the coast of Mongibello. There's a
maneuver going on with the sail. Captain Dickie supervises
his crew of Marge and a painfully awkward, anxious-to-
please Ripley. Dickie goes over to help him.

                    RIPLEY

I'm doing this wrong, aren't I?

                    DICKIE

You're doing great. We'll make a sailor of you
yet. You're doing really well.

                    MARGE

Dubious but special honor, Tom—crewing
Dickie's boat. All right, bar's open.

She heads for the cabin. Dickie settles down beside Ripley.

                    RIPLEY

Could we sail to Venice?

                    DICKIE

Sure. I love Venice.

                    RIPLEY

I have to go to Venice.

                    DICKIE

See Venice and die, isn't that right? Or is it
Rome? You do something and die, don't
you? Okay, Venice is on the list.

And Rome.

DICKIE

Do you ski?

(Ripley frowns)

Don't tell me—you're a lost cause! That's
the next thing to deal with. We're planning to
go to Cortina at Christmas. Excellent skiing.
Excellent.

(as Marge reappears)

Marge—Ripley can't ski. We'll have to teach
him that, too. Such low class, Marge, does
this guy know anything?

MARGE

Poor Tom. Good thing we're not getting
married. We might have to invite him on our
honeymoon.

EXT. MONGIBELLO. LATE DAY.

Marge and Ripley are on a shopping expedition. They walk
down the hill towards the grocery shop, next to the bar in the
little square. Ripley has asked Marge how she and Dickie met.

MARGE

Oh, I hated New York—that Park Avenue
crowd—so I fled to Paris to work on my
book, and I was always going to this cafe
with Jean-Jacques, and Dickie used to play
his saxophone outside and I would see him
and he would see me, and he would play *My
Funny Valentine.*

They've arrived at the Grocery Store. Alessandra, the woman
who owns the store, greets them. Silvana, who's her daugh-
ter, is also there, and less comfortable. She waits for Marge's
order.

MARGE (CONT'D)
(to Silvana, in Italian)

Buono sera, Silvana. Per favore: arance e pane, e del prosciutto.

SILVANA

E fichi? Come sempre.

MARGE

Si. Come sempre. Grazie.

Silvana goes inside for the meat and bread. Marge frowns.

MARGE (CONT'D)
(back to Ripley)

Anyway, then one day, we go in, I see Dickie, he starts playing *My Funny Valentine*, and then all of a sudden he just walks into the cafe, right in front of Jean-Jacques, and grabs me! Now I had never spoken to him in my life—he said *I'm going to Italy, tomorrow, and I want you to come with me.* So I did.
(of Silvana)
Does that girl look at me in a weird way? I think she does, doesn't she.

At the edge of the square there's A BOCCE AREA, where men throw metal balls along a track, aiming to get closest to a small cue. Dickie is there, playing intensely with Fausto and two other guys, one of whom we've seen before with Silvana. Ripley and Marge loop back towards home, taking in the bocce en route. Dickie waves. They wave back. Marge calls to him.

MARGE (CONT'D)

If you're not at my place by seven o'clock, Tom and I are running off together.

DICKIE

Okay.

— 30 —

EXT. MARGE'S HOUSE. EARLY EVENING.

Dickie and Ripley are leaving. They're fooling around.
Dickie jumps on Ripley's shoulders. Marge watches from the
top of the garden.

EXT. MONGIBELLO SQUARE. EARLY EVENING.

Dickie and Ripley, still horsing about, pass Silvana's grocery
store. Dickie dismounts, goes over to Silvana. They huddle,
Ripley isolated. Dickie takes an apple from a box, tosses it to
Ripley, as if they've stopped only for fruit, then turns back to
Silvana, who's tense, a little troubled. Their conversation is
sotto voce.

> SILVANA
>
> Did you get my message? I want to talk to
> you.

> DICKIE
>
> I want to talk to you, too...

> SILVANA
>
> I don't mean that kind of talk.

> DICKIE
>
> I can't now, your mother's coming.

And her mother appears; Silvana scowls her away, but
Dickie's already gone, back to Ripley, feinting to box him
then dancing, satyr-like, down the hill.

EXT. COASTAL ROAD TO NAPLES. EVENING.

Dickie and Ripley on the Vespa. There's a steep incline
where the road winds down towards Naples and, as the
Vespa gains speed, Ripley is happy to cling to Dickie.

> DICKIE
>
> You're breaking my ribs!

RIPLEY
What?

DICKIE

You're breaking my ribs!

INT. JAZZ CLUB, NAPLES. NIGHT.

Ripley's really singing, carrying the burden of *My Funny Valentine* in a flawless imitation of Chet Baker. Dickie is playing some sax. After a verse, there's spontaneous applause. Dickie, impressed, beams at Ripley.

INT. DICKIE'S HOUSE. NIGHT.

A NEW ICEBOX, incongruous in pride of place in the living room, casts its glow on a delighted Dickie as he pulls out a couple of beers, handing one to Ripley who is paging through his copy of the Collected Works of SHAKESPEARE.

DICKIE

I could fuck this icebox I love it so much.
(considering Ripley)
What were you actually doing in New York?

RIPLEY

I played piano in a few places.

DICKIE

That's one job, you told me a lot of jobs.

RIPLEY

A few places—that's a few jobs. Anyway, I
don't want to think about New York.

DICKIE

The mysterious Mr. Ripley. Marge and I
spend hours speculating.
(drinking)
Cold beer. Thank you, Dad.

RIPLEY

Copy out from here…

He hands the book to Dickie, pointing out the lines.

DICKIE

You bring this to Europe with you,
Shakespeare—that's so touching.

RIPLEY

Are you going to write something?

DICKIE
(starting to write on the back of a postcard)
I love the fact you brought Shakespeare with
you and no clothes. Ermelinda says you
wash the same shirt out every night. Is that
true?

RIPLEY

No! I've got more than one shirt!

DICKIE

She can do that stuff for you. Anyway, just
wear some of my things, wear anything you
want, most of it's ancient.
(he's finished writing)
Macbeth. Why this passage?

RIPLEY

Just something to write. Now your signature.
(watching him write)
Not "Dickie." Your signature.

Dickie writes his signature at the bottom of the postcard.
Ripley studies the writing, takes off his glasses to clean them.
Dickie looks at him.

DICKIE

Without the glasses you're not even ugly.

DICKIE (CONT'D)
(takes them, tries them on)
I don't need them because I never read.
How do I look?

RIPLEY
Like Clark Kent.
(takes them back, puts them on beaming at Dickie)
Now Superman.

Dickie cuffs him. Ripley looks down at the postcard.

DICKIE
I know. I write like a child.

RIPLEY
Pretty vile. See this: the **S** and the **T**, do you
see?—fine, vulnerable—that's pain, that's
secret pain.

DICKIE
It must be a deep secret, 'cause I don't know
about it.

RIPLEY
Your handwriting—nothing more naked.
See—nothing's quite touching the line—
that's vanity.

DICKIE
(flattered)
Well we certainly know that's true.

INT. DICKIE'S BATHROOM. NIGHT.

Dickie's in the bath. Ripley, dressed, sits on the stool next to
the bath. They're in the middle of playing chess, the board
propped on the bath tray. Ripley puts his hand in the water,
checking the temperature. He turns on the faucet for a burst
of hot. Ripley is absurdly happy. He pours some wine.

DICKIE
Do you have any brothers?

                        RIPLEY
No, no brothers, no sisters.

                        DICKIE
Me neither. Nor does Marge. All only children—what does that mean?

He looks at Ripley who looks at him, a little too long.

                        RIPLEY
Means we never shared a bath. I'm cold. Can
I get in?

                        DICKIE
No!

                        RIPLEY
I didn't mean with you in it.

                        DICKIE
                       (standing)
Okay, you get in. I'm like a prune anyway.

He gets out, walks past Ripley, who doesn't turn around. But
Dickie's reflected in the mirror. Ripley looks, then Dickie
turns, holds his look momentarily before flicking him with
his towel.

INT./EXT. AMERICAN EXPRESS OFFICE, NAPLES. DAY.

An OFFICIAL is studying Dickie's passport photograph. It's
not a recent picture. The official looks suspicious. Dickie is
used to it.

                        DICKIE
It is me. It's an old picture.
                   (sighs at Ripley)

Every time—"Is it you? Doesn't look like
you."

He's signing for his allowance. He has a smart document
case with his initials prominently embossed. Ripley watches
him sign and collect a large wad of notes.

CLERK

Letters—*Greenleaf*, and for *Ripley*.

Ripley collects and studies his mail. As they walk outside he
holds up one letter to Dickie.

RIPLEY

Fran.
(anticipating her letter)
I miss you, when are you coming home? Stop
telling me what a great time you're having,
how you love Dickie…and Marge and…
(the next letter)
And this one, I think, is your dad…

INT. TRAIN TO ROME. DAY.

Ripley sits reading the LETTER from Herbert Greenleaf. He
frowns, stops reading, looks out of the window.

DICKIE

What does he say?

RIPLEY

He's getting impatient. He's wants me to
reassure him you'll be home by
Thanksgiving.

DICKIE

You've got to get a new jacket. Really. You
must be sick of the same clothes. I'm sick of
seeing you in them.

RIPLEY

I can't. I can't keep spending your father's
money.

DICKIE

I love how responsible you are. My dad
should make you Chief Accountant or something.   Let me buy you a jacket. With my
money.   There's a great place when we get to
Rome, Batistoni.

Ripley is looking out of the window—his reflection hits
Dickie's. AS HE MOVES HIS FACE HE COVERS DICKIE'S
FACE WITH HIS OWN. He likes doing this. The train runs
on, ploughing up to Rome.

DICKIE   (CONT'D)
Andiamo a Roma. Andiamo, andiamo,
andiamo a Roma.

EXT. ARCARI'S CAFÉ, PIAZZA NAVONA, ROME. DAY.

Ripley and Dickie sit outside at a café in the Piazza Navona.
Very smart, very sophisticated, very young crowd. There are
already several empty coffee cups and a half empty bottle of
Frascati. Ripley has his guidebook out and is incredibly impatient. Dickie, meanwhile, has stretched out for the duration.

RIPLEY

Where do we find a carozza for the Forum,
or can we hire any of them—?

DICKIE

Relax.

RIPLEY

It's just there's so much to do in a single day.

DICKIE

Relax. You'll find out more about Rome sitting here than plodding around the Coliseum behind a busload of hausfrau. The most important question is where to eat. I hope Freddie made a reservation.

RIPLEY

Freddie?

DICKIE

Freddie Miles. You know—he's organizing the Cortina skiing trip.

Ripley hates the idea of having this special day invaded. A horn makes him look up as FREDDIE MILES illegally parks his open-topped sports car opposite the cafe, sees Dickie and bustles over. He's a heavy-set American with a reddish crewcut. Ripley finds him disgusting to look at. Dickie is delighted.

DICKIE

Frederico!

FREDDIE

Ciao bello.
(noticing a beautiful woman in an open-topped car)
Don't you want to fuck every woman you see? Just once.

They kiss cheeks, Continental-style.

DICKIE

This is Tom Ripley. Freddie Miles.

FREDDIE
(mugging)
Hey, if I'm late, think what her husband's saying!

He fills Dickie's glass with wine and drinks it standing up.

So let's go. I got us a table outside at
Fabrizio's.

And Dickie's up, leaving Ripley to pick up all the tiny checks
to work out the bill and pay it.

DICKIE

I'll tell you—I am so cabin-crazy with Mongi.

Freddie and Dickie link arms Italian-style and cross the street
to Freddie's car.

FREDDIE

I know. I was there.
(looks back to see Ripley struggling to settle the check)
Tommy! It's S.R.O. Two seater. Standing
Room Only. Chop, chop, Tommy!

Ripley, abandoned, goes over. There's no room in the car. He
has to crouch in the rear.

FREDDIE (CONT'D)

You're going to have to sit between us. But
don't put your shoes on the seat, know what
I mean, put them on top of each other.
Okay?

INT. A JAZZ RECORD STORE. LATE AFTER-NOON.

This record store is hidden away down a cobbled alley, and
stuffed with the trendiest Romans, all of whom riffle the
stacks under a fog of cigarette smoke. There are two LIS-
TENING BOOTHS, one of which has Freddie and Dickie
crammed into it, sharing a set of headphones. Ripley stands
outside the booth, holding both of their jackets like a manser-
vant, while inside and behind the glass doors they chat ani-
matedly. He looks longingly at the street, where the light is

fading. Dickie catches his hangdog expression and pushes open the accordion doors.

> **DICKIE**
>
> Look, Tom, we've got to go to a club and meet some friends of Freddie's. The best thing is— if you want to be a tourist—grab a cab and we can meet up at the railway station.

> **RIPLEY**
> *(absolutely crestfallen)*

What club?

> **DICKIE**
>
> Freddie's arranged it with some of the skiing crowd. Come if you want but I thought you wanted to see the Forum…?

> **RIPLEY**

I did. And then maybe get the jacket and what have you…

> **FREDDIE**
> *(from inside the booth)*

Dick—you've got to hear this!

> **DICKIE**
> *(oblivious to Ripley's pain)*

Listen, just take one of mine when we get back. Don't worry about it. I did the Forum with Marge and, frankly, once is enough in anyone's life.

Ripley hands him the coats, turns away.

> **DICKIE**

Ciao. Have fun.

Ripley heads for the door, then comes back, raps on the booth. Dickie pushes it open.

RIPLEY

You said to make sure you didn't miss the
train. It leaves at eight.

EXT. THE CAPITOL. LATE AFTERNOON.

Ripley hikes up Michelangelo's Arcoeli Steps. Then he's
looking down from the Campodoglio at the Forum below.
Then he's walking by the oversized fragments of the
Colossus. This is the real Ripley, the lover of beauty, inspired
by art, by antiquity. He's awed. He's cold. He so much wishes he weren't alone.

INT. ROME RAILWAY STATION. NIGHT.

It's past eight, Ripley stands, one foot on the guard step of
the Naples train, waiting forlornly for Dickie, then giving up
as the train pulls away. He pulls the door to his compartment
closed, and sits inside the train alone.

INT. DICKIE'S BEDROOM. NIGHT.

There's music playing, Bing Crosby's *May I*. Very loud.
Ripley dances to the mirror, SPECTACLES ABANDONED and
IN HIS TUXEDO MINUS TROUSERS. He adjusts his hair,
catches one of Dickie's expressions. There are clothes abandoned everywhere. He's been having a big dressing-up session. He sings along with Bing.

DICKIE (O/S)

What are you doing?

Ripley turns, horrified, to see Dickie standing in the doorway. The music thumps away.

RIPLEY

Oh—just amusing myself. Sorry, Dickie.

(pause)

RIPLEY (CONT'D)

I didn't think you were coming back.

Dickie turns off the record player.

DICKIE

I wish you'd get out of my clothes.

Ripley starts undressing, his fingers clumsy with mortification and shock. Dickie looks at his feet, shakes his head.

DICKIE

Do you have my shoes on too?

RIPLEY
(lame, ashamed)

You said I could pick out a jacket and I just… Sorry.

DICKIE

Get undressed in your own room, would you?

RIPLEY

I thought you'd missed the train.

DICKIE

Freddie drove me back in his car.

RIPLEY
(horrified)

Is Freddie here?

DICKIE

He's downstairs.

RIPLEY

I was just fooling around. Don't say anything. Sorry.

Dickie lets him leave and then sits amongst the debris of the dressing-up session, not amused.

INT. RIPLEY'S BEDROOM. NIGHT.

Ripley is in bed, in his pyjamas. He hears Freddie's distinctive laugh downstairs.

EXT. DICKIE'S TERRACE. DAY.

Ripley comes down, apprehensive, to find Marge and Dickie and Freddie having a jolly breakfast on the terrace. Dickie looks perfectly happy.

> MARGE
>
> Hi, Tom. Come join us.

> RIPLEY
>
> Morning.

> FREDDIE
>
> You should have waited last night. You could have come back with us in the car.

> RIPLEY
>
> Waited where? I didn't know there was a plan...

> DICKIE
>
> There was no plan. Tom always likes a plan.

> RIPLEY
>
> No, I don't.

> FREDDIE
>
> I want this job of yours, Tommy. I was just saying—You live in Italy, sleep in Dickie's house, eat Dickie's food, wear his clothes, and his father picks up the tab. If you get bored, let me know, I'll do it!

> DICKIE
> *(trying to alleviate Ripley's anxiety)*
>
> He means my jacket.
>
> *(as if to Marge)*
>
> I'm giving Tom a jacket.

> **MARGE**
> *(to Ripley's defense)*
> That's not quite fair. We made Tom stay
> here, and we turned him into our Double
> Agent, didn't we?—and the icebox—which is
> a godsend—Tom bought that.

> **FREDDIE**
> Cool.

EXT. THE OCEAN, ABOARD THE *BIRD*. DAY.

The boat is drifting. Freddie and Dickie and Marge are swimming, then Marge climbs back onto the boat, where Ripley is sitting alone, reading.

> **MARGE**
> You really should go in, it's marvelous.

> **RIPLEY**
> I'm fine.

She approaches him, conscious of his isolation. She's in a red bikini, and she towels herself dry as they speak.

> **MARGE**
> Are you okay?

> **RIPLEY**
> Sure.

They watch Dickie and Freddie fooling around in the water.

> **MARGE**
> The thing with Dickie—it's like the sun
> shines on you and it's glorious, then he for-
> gets you and it's very very cold.

> **RIPLEY**
> So I'm learning.

> **MARGE**
> He's not even aware of it. When you've got

MARGE (CONT'D)

his attention you feel like you're the only person in the world. That's why everybody loves
him. Other times…

There's a yell from Dickie as Freddie wrestles with him.

DICKIE
(laughing and choking)

He's drowning me!

MARGE

It's always the same whenever someone new
comes into his life—Freddie, Fausto, Peter
Smith-Kingsley—he's wonderful—did you
meet him, he's a musician?…and especially
you, of course…and that's only the boys.

They watch as Freddie pushes Dickie under the surface.

MARGE

Tell me, why is it when men play they always
play at killing each other…? I'm sorry about
Cortina, by the way.

RIPLEY

What about Cortina?

MARGE

Didn't Dick say? He talked to Freddie…
apparently it's not going to work out—
Freddie says there aren't enough rooms.
(Ripley's devastated, Marge notices, can't look at him)
Keep it up Freddie, there are still signs of life!!

EXT. OCEAN, ABOARD THE *BIRD*. DUSK.

LATER and now the boat is sailing again. Ripley is sitting in
his spot. Dickie and Freddie are at the tiller.

DICKIE

Come on, Frederico, do you really have to

DICKIE (CONT'D)

go back? At least stick around for the festival. It's great, the Festival of the Madonna?

FREDDIE

I don't think so. Come back with me to
Rome. There's this great new club. Have
some drinks, lotta ladies...

Marge, still in her bikini, disappears into the cabin. Dickie
makes a face at Freddie.

DICKIE

Do you think you can steer this thing?

FREDDIE

Sure.

DICKIE

Just point her at Capri and avoid the rocks.

FREDDIE

What are you doing?

DICKIE

Marge-maintenance.

FREDDIE

Aye, aye.

Dickie heads towards the cabin. Freddie takes over the tiller.
There's a breeze and the sailboat cuts through the water.

From where Ripley sits he can see Capri in the distance, but
he can also look down into the cabin, its porthole offering
him a restricted view. He looks down and there's a flash of
flesh, then nothing. Then as the boat swings with the waves,
he glimpses the bikini top flung over a chair, and then
Marge's bare foot kicking out rhythmically, the red-painted
toes straining. Ripley's mesmerized, aroused and absolutely
betrayed.

FREDDIE
(calling out)

Tommy—how's the peeping! Come on
Tommy, you were looking. Tommy, Tommy,
Tommy.

Shamed, Ripley looks away. He stares at the water, parting
before the boat, its turmoil reflecting his.

EXT. DICKIE'S MOORING. DAY.

The *Bird* returns to the mooring by Dickie's house. Dickie,
as ever Captain of the Ship, clambering around, shouting
instructions, with Ripley, Marge and Freddie as crew. Ripley
looks back at shore. Silvana stands watching, staring. Dickie
notices her too.

EXT. MONGIBELLO SLIPWAY. LATE DAY.

A WOMAN'S HEAD suddenly breaks the surface of the water.

It's a statue of the Virgin Mary, life-size, adorned with flowers
and a lace veil. As she is revealed, wooden, staring, four men
emerge, lifting the statue on a palette, wading towards the
shore, the Madonna aloft on their shoulders.

The whole town of Mongibello is in attendance for this
Annual Festival of the Madonna del Mare, either standing in
their fishing boats, or on shore and flanking the Parish Priest
and altar boys and incense. RIPLEY, DICKIE and MARGE
watch from Dickie's terrace. There are hymns and, as the
statue is carried to the shore, the men's heads barely above
the waves, the congregation applauds at the illusion that the
Madonna is walking on water.

Suddenly ANOTHER HEAD appears on the surface of the
water, about fifty yards from the statue. There's a scream

from among the crowd as someone notices the body. It's SIL-VANA. One of the MEN carrying the statue turns first towards the direction of the scream and then towards the floating corpse. It's Silvana's fiancé, and in a second he has let go of the palette, CAUSING IT TO TOPPLE, and—in absolute grief —wades, swims, splashes towards the body.

PANDEMONIUM in the crowd, which breaks up, with other people splashing, fully clothed, into the water. From the ter-race, Ripley turns and looks at Dickie, catching his eye.

EXT. DICKIE'S TERRACE. LATE DAY.

Marge and Ripley and Dickie watch from the terrace as below them an AMBULANCE takes away the body. It seems as if the whole town looks on—fiancé, parents, brothers, sisters, police, priest, etc. As the corpse is loaded into the vehicle A BRIEF SCUFFLE occurs between Silvana's fiancé and her brother. They are pulled apart. Then the ambulance pulls away.

> **RIPLEY**
> What's the fight about? That's her fiancé, isn't it? Are they blaming him?

> **DICKIE**
> *(sharp)*
> I don't know! Why are you asking me?
> *(agitated)*
> How can it take an hour to find an ambu-lance?

> **MARGE**
> *(conciliatory)*
> Well, she was already dead, darling, wasn't she, so I suppose—

> **DICKIE**
> I don't know why people say this country's civilized. It isn't. It's fucking primitive.

And with that HE KICKS OUT VIOLENTLY AT A CHAIR
SUPPORTING THE RECORD PLAYER. Records, machine,
chair go flying into the open room. Dickie follows them.

> **MARGE**
> Dickie!

> **RIPLEY**
> I'll go and see what's the matter.

> **MARGE**
> I'll go.

INT. DICKIE'S HOUSE. LATE AFTERNOON.

Later, Dickie is slumped in an armchair at the open window
overlooking the slipway. He's playing sax. A forlorn, keening
phrase from *You Don't Know What Love Is*. Ripley appears,
begins tidying the mess of the living room. He picks up broken records, the chair Dickie has kicked at, its leg broken. He
examines the damage.

> **RIPLEY**
> I know why you're upset.
> *(Dickie continues playing)*
> I know about Silvana, Dickie. About you and
> Silvana.

Dickie stops playing.

> **DICKIE**
> What about us?

Ripley now has an armful of dishes and glasses and bottles.

> **DICKIE**
> You don't have to clean up! Really.
> Ermelinda will do that in the morning.

Ripley disappears into the kitchen.

> **D I C K I E (CONT'D)**
> *(as Ripley returns)*

She was pregnant. Did you know that? Do
you know what that means in a place like
this?

> **R I P L E Y**

I'm prepared to take the blame.

> **D I C K I E**

What are you talking about?

> **R I P L E Y**

You've been so good to me. You're the brother I never had. I'm the brother you never
had.

> **D I C K I E**

She came to me for help, she needed money,
and I didn't help her. I didn't help her. Now
she's dead and it's my fault. And you can't
change that.

> **R I P L E Y**

I'm not going to say anything—to Marge, or
anybody, the police— It's a secret between us
and I'll keep it.

And he disappears again, leaving Dickie to resume the sax,
somehow in thrall to Ripley.

> **R I P L E Y (O/S)**
> *Dear Tom, I think the time has come to dis-
> continue your expense checks...*

EXT. AMERICAN EXPRESS, NAPLES. DAY.

Ripley and Dickie are walking out of the American Express
Office, Dickie pushing the rest of his money into his case,
Ripley—despondent—reading aloud extracts from a letter
from Herbert Greenleaf—

RIPLEY

...The thousand dollars, of course, was only due in the event that you succeeded in bringing Dickie home. Naturally, I hope the trip has afforded you some pleasure despite the failure of its main objective. You need no longer consider yourself obligated to us in any way...

DICKIE

You can't blame him. You could hardly expect this to go on forever.

RIPLEY

I thought you might write again. Now that we're brothers...

DICKIE

I can't, how can I, in all decency? We've had a good run, haven't we?

RIPLEY
(increasingly miserable)

What about Venice? Can we stick to that plan at least?

DICKIE

I don't think so, Tom. You can't stay on here without money. It's time we all moved on. Besides, I'm sick of Mongi. Especially now with everything—I really want to move to the north. I need to check out San Remo next week, find somewhere new to keep the boat. But it would be great, though, if you came with me. Our last trip before you leave. What do you think? A last trip?

INT. TRAIN TO SAN REMO. AFTERNOON.

Dickie and Ripley travel up to San Remo. They sit next to

each other. Dickie's asleep. Ripley almost lays his head on Dickie's shoulder, but when he makes to do that, Dickie stirs. Then Ripley plays his familiar game of studying his face in the reflection of the train window, so that he can move his head and see his reflection, then back and see Dickie's. Dickie suddenly catches him staring. Ripley looks away.

> DICKIE
> *(terse)*
>
> Why do you do that thing—with your neck? On trains you always do that thing, it's so spooky.

EXT. HOTEL TERRACE RESTAURANT, SAN REMO. NIGHT.

Dickie and Ripley walk through the terrace of a hotel which lips out towards the sea. There's a restaurant and palms and a JAZZ QUINTET playing, American. Very cool. They pass the band. Dickie's captivated as they head for their table. They pass some girls at a table. Dickie smiles greedily.

> DICKIE
>
> This is more like it. Didn't I tell you San Remo was crazy!

They're shown to a good table. Dickie watches the band while their glasses are filled with champagne. Ripley looks happy. He's got Dickie all to himself.

> RIPLEY
>
> To Mongibello and the happiest days of my life.

> DICKIE
>
> To Mongi. You're cheerful tonight.

> RIPLEY
>
> I'm suddenly quite happy to be going back.

DICKIE

That's good.

RIPLEY

I've got plans!

DICKIE

Ripley's plans.

RIPLEY

Esatto. I'm always planning.

DICKIE

Did I know you at Princeton, Tom? I didn't, did I?

RIPLEY

Why are you asking all of a sudden?

DICKIE

No reason. Because you're leaving, I guess. I don't think you were there, were you?

RIPLEY

Why?

DICKIE

I mean it as a compliment. You've got such great taste, I don't know. Most of the thugs at Princeton had tasted everything and had no taste. Used to say, the cream of America: Rich and thick. Freddie's the perfect example.

RIPLEY

Then I'll take it as a compliment.

DICKIE

I knew it! I had a bet with Marge!

RIPLEY
(a beat)

Ha.

DICKIE

Do you even like jazz—or was that something
for my benefit?

RIPLEY
(conceding, without guile)

I've gotten to like it. I've gotten to like everything about the way you live. It's one big love
affair. If you knew my life back home in New
York...

Dickie's distracted by the drummer who's playing an extro-
vert solo, doesn't hear the confession of love.

DICKIE

I'm thinking of giving up the sax, what do
you think about drums?

RIPLEY

What?

DICKIE

So cool.

He mimes a high-hat and snare. Ripley can't quite credit this
—its superficiality.

EXT. MID-OCEAN. DAY.

The bay of San Remo. DICKIE and RIPLEY have hired a
motorboat.

DICKIE

That's how I found my place in Mongi.
Took a boat out round the bay. The first
place I liked, I got it.

The motorboat is ploughing the waves. Dickie exhilarated by
the speed.

RIPLEY

Dickie, slow down, come on!

Ripley grips the oar, his knuckles white. Dickie cuts the motor, and the boat slows to a crawl, miles from the shore.

> **D I C K I E**
> *(ecstatic)*
> I love it here! Gonna live here!

Dickie takes off his jacket, then drums against the edge of the boat, developing a rhythm with his lighter and fingers, already on the way to becoming Buddy Rich.

> **R I P L E Y**
> I wanted to tell you my plan.

> **D I C K I E**
> So tell me.

> **R I P L E Y**
> I thought I might come back. In the new year. Under my own steam.

> **D I C K I E**
> *(suddenly tight)*
> Really? To Italy?

> **R I P L E Y**
> Of course. Let's say, for argument's sake, you were here—perhaps we could split the rent on a house—I'll get a job—or, better still, I could get a place in Rome and when we're there we could be there and if we're here we could be here—

> **D I C K I E**
> Oh God, I don't think so.

> **R I P L E Y**
> —you see, particularly with the Marge problem, you can just blame me.

> **D I C K I E**
> Marge and I are getting married.

                    RIPLEY
                   (appalled)
How?

                    DICKIE
How?

                    RIPLEY
Yesterday you're ogling girls on the terrace,
today you're getting married. It's absurd.

                    DICKIE
I love Marge.

                    RIPLEY
You love me and you're not marrying me.

                    DICKIE
                    (cold)
Tom, I don't love you.

                    RIPLEY
No, no, it's not a threat, I've explained all of
that.

                    DICKIE
I'm actually a little relieved you're going, to
be honest. I think we've seen enough of each
other for a while.

Ripley stares at him, his eyes suddenly reptilian.

                    RIPLEY
What?

                    DICKIE
You can be a leech—you know this—and it's
boring. You can be quite boring.

                    RIPLEY
                   (volcanic)
The funny thing—*I'm* not pretending to be
somebody else and you are. I'm absolutely

honest with you. I've told you my feelings.
But you, first of all I know there's something
—that evening when we played chess, for
instance, it was obvious—

DICKIE
(incredulous)

What evening?

RIPLEY

Sure—I know, that's too dangerous for you,
fair enough, hey! We're brothers, fine, then
you do this sordid thing with Marge, fucking
her on the boat while we all have to listen,
which was excruciating, frankly, plus you follow your cock around like a—and now you're
getting married! I'm bewildered, forgive
me…you're lying to Marge then getting married to her, you're knocking up Silvana, you've
got to play sax, you've got to play drums,
which is it, Dickie, what do you really play?

Dickie, furious, gets up, and lurches towards Ripley.

DICKIE
*(attacking him, administering tiny slaps as
punctuation to his tirade)*

Who are you—some imposter, some third-
class mooch—who are you to tell me anything? Actually, I really really really don't
want to be on this boat with you, I can't
move without you moving, which is exactly
how it feels and it gives me the creeps.
(he goes to rev up the engine)
I can't move without "Dickie, Dickie,
Dickie"—like a little girl. You give me the—

RIPLEY SMASHES HIM ACROSS THE HEAD WITH THE
OAR. DICKIE SLIPS OFF THE WOODEN SEAT, HIS EYES
ROLLING IN GROGGY SURPRISE.

R I P L E Y

Shut up! Just shut up! Just shut up!

The boat slows as Dickie releases the tiller. Dickie looks up
at Ripley wearily and slides onto his back.

D I C K I E

For God's sake.

Ripley, shocked at himself, goes to Dickie, rocking the boat,
catches him up, then is horrified to see Dickie's face, apparently unmarked, SUDDENLY SPLIT OPEN, a line of blood and
then a peeling like a fruit bursting. Ripley's appalled. A terrible roar issues from Dickie as he launches himself at Ripley.

D I C K I E (CONT'D)

I'll kill you!

Ripley finds himself pushing him away, picking up the oar,
kicking off Dickie's hand around his ankle. The boat is rocking
and swerving crazily as Dickie falls against the tiller. Ripley
almost loses his balance. His glasses come off. They struggle,
locked together in a life or death wrestle to get control of the
oar. Dickie, blinded by his own blood, loses his grip.

Ripley, terrified, hits Dickie again and again, the oar like a
carpet beater banging down flat, blood on the blade, blood
on Ripley, until he's on his knees, heaving for breath, letting
his arm drop, then realizing, disgusted, that he's let it rest in
a pool of blood. He starts to sob, sprawls there, sobbing, next
to Dickie, horrified by what he's done.

Nobody's in sight. The boat rocks, gently, the sun sparkling
indifferently on the waves. Ripley lies by Dickie in the bottom of the boat, in the embrace he's always wanted.

Later and Ripley's tied the rope attached to the anchor around Dickie's bare ankles in a huge and overelaborate knot.

HE HEAVES THE ANCHOR OVER. It sinks through the transparent water, drawing the rope taut on Dickie's ankle, Ripley is helping, lifting up the legs, and when the heavy part of the body sticks at the gunwale, it takes an almighty effort to get the body over the side.

The pretty blue-and-white boat rocks peacefully. The sea calms.

EXT. A COVE NEAR SAN REMO. AFTERNOON.

A deserted cove, several miles along the coast.

Ripley piles rocks into the boat, then leans on the hull, rocking it full of water.

He clambers onto a rock over the shore. He's watching the boat slowly sinking. Shuddering from the exertion, the cold, he finds Dickie's jacket, puts it on and watches as the boat disappears under the surface.

EXT. SAN REMO. DUSK.

Ripley walks back towards the hotel, still wearing Dickie's jacket, cold and wet, his bag over his shoulder.

INT. HOTEL LOBBY. EARLY EVENING.

Ripley approaches the front desk. He's shivering. He's not wearing his glasses.

RIPLEY

Can I have my key, please?

RECEPTIONIST
(at the key rack)

Of course—Signor Greenleaf? Yes?—But you must be very cold?

RIPLEY

No, it's—I'm...
                    (mind racing)
No, I was going to say no I'm not cold, but
now I realize I am. I'm frozen. Can you pre-
pare my bill, please, and also Mr. Ripley's?
We're checking out.

RECEPTIONIST
(concerned)
Oh?

RIPLEY

Mr. Ripley met a pretty girl on the beach—
French, from Paris, so...

RECEPTIONIST
(knowingly)
Ah, Paris. No sister?

RIPLEY

No sister.

EXT. ROAD BETWEEN NAPLES AND MONGI-BELLO. DAY.

Ripley sits on the bus as it rumbles towards Mongi. He
stares out of the window, full of what he's done. No idea what
to do.

EXT. MONGIBELLO, FISHERMAN'S WHARF. DAY.

The BUS comes into town. Ripley gets out, looks calm, very
together.

INT. DICKIE'S LIVING ROOM. DAY.

Ripley walks into the living room, slowly approaches
Dickie's saxophone which is on its stand on the table. He
can't get close to it, it evokes Dickie too much.

INT. DICKIE'S BEDROOM. DAY.

Ripley is in Dickie's bedroom. Evidence of Dickie every-where, photographs, clothes, shoes. Ripley is sitting on the floor, weeping into a pillow.

INT. DICKIE'S LIVING ROOM, MONGIBELLO. DAY.

Ripley has Dickie's Hermés Baby typewriter on the desk and is busy writing letters. He has finished a letter to the Greenleafs, now he's at the end of one to Marge. We can read part of it: *C/O American Express, Rome 9 November 1958. Dear Marge, this is a difficult letter for me to write…* Ripley produces the Shakespeare and Signature page and COPIES DICKIE'S SIGNATURE at the end of the letter.

EXT. MARGE'S GARDEN, MONGIBELLO. DAY.

Ripley stands at the entrance to Marge's garden where she is working at her book on the outside table, surrounded by ref-erences and notes, held down by bricks. He looks at her until she looks at him. She's startled, gasps.

> RIPLEY
>
> Hello, Marge.

> MARGE
>
> Tom, you startled me! You're back.

> RIPLEY
>
> How are you? Sorry. Is your book going well?

> MARGE
>
> Yes—I'm on a good streak, thanks.

> RIPLEY
>
> I was just looking at you—
> *(looking at her tenderly)*
> —so quiet.

MARGE

Where's Dickie?

RIPLEY

I think he's planning on staying in Rome for
a few days.

MARGE
(looks at him)

Ha. Did he say why?

RIPLEY

I don't know. I don't understand Dickie,
Marge, so your guess is as good as mine.

MARGE

What does that mean?

RIPLEY

Well, one day I'm invited skiing, the next day
I'm not, one day we're all one family, the next
day he wants to be alone. You tell me.

MARGE

Is that what he said—he wanted to be alone?

RIPLEY

He was thinking of you, Marge—he asked me
to deliver this.

He hands her a package. She pulls at it, it's perfume.

MARGE

Thanks. He knows I love this, although why
it couldn't have waited...

RIPLEY

Errand number one—deliver Marge's perfume. Errand number two, pack some
clothes and his precious saxophone.

MARGE
(alarmed)

How long's he staying for?

> **RIPLEY**
> Search me. I guess we're abandoned.

> **MARGE**
> Are you going to Rome?

> **RIPLEY**
> *(turning to leave)*
> I'm going home, back to New York. Maybe
> through Venice, but I'll stop off with his
> things, yes, on the way.

EXT. MONGIBELLO, BEACH. EARLY MORNING.

Marge is walking along the beach and out onto the jetty, forlorn, a bleached figure on this winter morning.

INT. OFF FROM DICKIE'S LIVING ROOM. MORNING.

As Ripley walks down the stairs, Marge is at the icebox in the
living room. She's fixing herself a drink, has the icebox open
for ice. She's ashen, and might have been weeping, walks
back into the kitchen area.

> **MARGE**
> I just got a letter from Dickie. You realize it's more
> than a few days? He's thinking of *moving* to Rome.

She bangs out the ice onto the counter, cubes falling everywhere. Ripley drops to the floor and starts to clear them up.
She's got the letter, shows it to Ripley.

> **MARGE**
> He's just impossible. He can't even write the
> envelope. World's worst handwriting.

Ripley puts fresh ice into her glass.

> **MARGE**
> The thing is, the night before he left, we
> talked about moving, together, going north,

Porto Ercole or somewhere, anyway leaving
Mongi—and I suppose I put some pressure
on him, about getting married, and I'm just—
I just must have scared him off.

Ripley lights a cigarette.

MARGE

Dickie says I should take the icebox to my
place, by the way.

RIPLEY

Right.

MARGE

It's turning so cold now I don't need it.

INT. ALBERGO GOLDONI, ROME. DAY.

RIPLEY'S BATTERED CASES are carried into the tiny lobby
of this small hotel. He exchanges his passport at the desk for
his room key, then makes his way, carrying his own luggage to
the metal cage elevator. THIS SCENE INTERCUTS WITH:

INT. HOTEL GRAND. DAY.

DICKIE'S ARRAY OF LEATHER LUGGAGE is pulled along on
a baggage trolley by a liveried PORTER.

Dickie's passport slides across the marble desk. A key comes
back, collected by a hand sporting Dickie's two distinctive
rings. As ALDO, the Front Desk Manager, inspects the passport, he looks at the owner. Ripley wears a terrific suit, his
hair parted in the Greenleaf style, no glasses. His voice, when
he speaks, has the same, lazy, confident drawl.

ALDO

Welcome back, Signor Greenleaf.

RIPLEY
(walking away)

Thank you.

INT. RIPLEY'S SUITE. GRAND. DAY.

The PORTER takes the cases and opens them as Ripley walks around the suite. It's large and splendid. Ripley breathes in its opulence. He immediately picks up the telephone.

> RIPLEY
>
> Yes, I'd like you to telephone the Hotel Goldoni. Yes. I want to speak to Signor Thomas Ripley—No, *R*ipley, R, yes. *Grazie.*

He produces Dickie's pen and signs the blotter quickly— *H R Greenleaf.* Then he pulls out a postcard from the writing case to reveal Dickie's *Stars, hide your fires* handwriting specimen. He compares the two signatures, is pleased.

The telephone rings.

> RIPLEY
>
> *Pronto?* Signor Ripley is not there? I'd like to leave a message. Yes. Please call Dickie—*Dickie Greenleaf* —at the Grand.

INT. RIPLEY'S HOTEL ROOM. GOLDONI. DAY.

A tiny cell of a room, single bed. Ripley on the phone.

> RIPLEY
>
> He's not there? Very well. I'll leave a mes-sage—*Got your call. Dinner tonight sounds fine. Ripley.*
>> *(listens as it's read back)*
> Dinner tonight, yes, is okay. Yes, thank you.

INT. GUCCI STORE, ROME. DAY.

Ripley has bought some more LEATHER GOODS—a brief-

case and overnight bag. He is at the counter, signing
checks.

> RIPLEY
>
> I'd like these to have my initials—embossed,
> I don't know the word in Italian…
> embossed?

> GUCCI ASSISTANT
>
> Embossed, of course, Signor Greenleaf.

There's an excited rap on the window and a shout of DICK-
IE! Shocked, Ripley looks over to find MEREDITH LOGUE
outside, alone and delighted to see him. He grins and
mouths hello.

> MEREDITH
> *(entering the shop)*
>
> Dickie! Oh my God! *Ciao.*

EXT. ACROSS PIAZZA NAVONA TO ARCARI'S CAFÉ. DAY.

Ripley and Meredith walk across the Piazza towards the café.

> MEREDITH
>
> But you're going skiing with us Yankees,
> aren't you?

> RIPLEY
>
> What?

> MEREDITH
>
> At Christmas. To Cortina with Freddie Miles
> and—

> RIPLEY
> *(interrupting, astonished)*
>
> How did you know that?

> MEREDITH
>
> Everybody knows Freddie Miles.

RIPLEY
(unsettled)

Is Freddie in Rome?

MEREDITH

Now? I don't think so. But I've met him, of
course, and we've chatted and I know about
you and Marge and Mongi and what an unre-
liable rat you are. Freddie said you were a rat
and I thought to myself now I know why he
travels under R.

RIPLEY

I've left Marge, Meredith. And Mongi. So the
rat's here now, in Rome.

MEREDITH

Sorry, I wouldn't have made a joke if—

RIPLEY

Don't be sorry. I've never been happier. I feel
like I've been handed a new life.

EXT. AMERICAN EXPRESS OFFICE, ROME.
DAY.

Meredith and Ripley walk down the Spanish Steps and head
inside the office.

MEREDITH

The truth is if you've had money your entire
life, even if you despise it, which we do—
agreed?—you're only truly comfortable
around other people who have it and despise
it.

RIPLEY

I know.

MEREDITH

I've never admitted that to anyone.

— 67 —

INT. AMERICAN EXPRESS OFFICE, ROME. DAY.

Ripley's signing Dickie's allowance receipt. Meredith is with him, signing her own counterfoil. He is, of course, endorsed by her presence. She goes to the window ahead of him.

She takes her money, turns to him.

He hands over his documents. The Clerk compares Ripley's signature with the one on the passport and then looks up at him. Ripley is cool as cucumber.

> RIPLEY
>
> I don't want too many large bills. Nobody
> will change them.

INT. RIPLEY'S SUITE, GRAND. ANOTHER DAY.

Where A TAILOR is finishing the fitting of a cashmere jacket for Ripley. Bolts of cloth everywhere as Meredith adjudicates the possible materials, which the tailor holds up against Ripley.

> MEREDITH
>
> Show me the other one again.
> *(the Tailor obliges)*
> I like them both.

> RIPLEY
>
> I'll take them both.

Ripley goes inside the bedroom to change. While he's inside, the Tailor leaves and Meredith opens the sax case, peers inside, holds up the instrument:

> MEREDITH (V/O)
>
> I know you're a jazz fiend but do you
> absolutely hate the opera? I've been trying
> to give my tickets away, it's tomorrow, but if
> you were prepared to be dragged...

She looks up to catch him bare-chested. She's intoxicated by
him, the romance she feels to be in the air.

> RIPLEY
> *(emerging)*

You could drag me.

INT. THE OPERA HOUSE. ROME.

On stage is Act Two of Eugene Onegin. Lensky sings his
aria before the duel with Onegin.

Ripley's in a tuxedo, in a box which includes a glamorous
Meredith and her AUNT AND UNCLE. He knows what
comes next. Lensky is shot by Onegin. Blood pours from his
neck into the snow. Onegin, horrified at the death of his
friend, goes over, wraps Lensky in his cloak, the silk lining
flashing, kneels holding him... Ripley can barely hide his
emotion... Meredith watches her sensitive friend, entranced.

INT. OUTSIDE THE BOXES, OPERA HOUSE.

The Interval. Ripley and Meredith exit their box with
Meredith's Aunt and Uncle (who heads for the interval
drinks).

> RIPLEY

Thanks so much for inviting me tonight.

> JOAN

Can you bear it? We hear you're a friend of
Freddie's—he has *I hate Opera* tattooed on
his chest.

> RIPLEY

There's room for a whole libretto on
Freddie's chest.

> JOAN
> *(laughs)*

I'm sure we've met.

They reach the console where Uncle Ted has their drinks.

> **J O A N**
> I was sure we'd met, weren't you, Ted? This
> is Herbert Greenleaf's boy.

> **R I P L E Y**
> Thanks, yes, I think we did.

> **J O A N**
> One minute you people are children and the
> next you're getting tattooed.

INT. OPERA HOUSE. FOYER. NIGHT.

Ripley heads past the Beautiful People on his hunt for
the Men's Room, and walks straight into MARGE. She's
talking to a young and cultured Englishman: PETER SMITH-
KINGSLEY.

> **M A R G E**
> *(as if she's seen a ghost)*
> Oh my god. Tom.

> **R I P L E Y**
> Marge, how are you? What are you doing in
> Rome?

> **M A R G E**
> Is he here? Are you with Dickie?

> **R I P L E Y**
> No.
> *(to Smith-Kingsley)*
> Hello, I'm Tom Ripley.

> **P E T E R**
> Peter Smith-Kingsley. I've heard about you,
> of course—from Marge, and Dickie.

> **M A R G E**
> *(works out what's strange)*
> No glasses.

He fishes out his glasses.

> RIPLEY
> *(to Peter)*

Ditto.

> PETER

Where are you hiding him? He's impossible, isn't he?

> MARGE

Is he really not here?

> RIPLEY

Marge, you know Dickie has *I hate Opera* tattooed on his chest.

> MARGE

You were going to Venice.

> PETER

Yes, what happened? I heard you were desperate to come. I was looking forward to rowing you around.

> RIPLEY

I am. I really am. And I've been traveling. I just can't seem to get that far north.

> PETER

Well hurry, before we sink.
> *(reaches into his jacket)*
Should I give you my telephone number in Venice?

> RIPLEY

Thanks.

The INTERVAL BELL'S ringing. Peter hands over his card to Ripley, sees Meredith.

> PETER

Look there's Meredith…the—who's that,

PETER (CONT'D)

Marge? they're in textiles…Meredith—
(embarrassed at not remembering)
God, how awful, I've spent Christmas in her
house…!

MARGE

I don't know her.
(to Ripley)
He hasn't called, he's hardly written, just
these cryptic notes. You don't just dump
people.

The last INTERVAL BELL. There's a mini-stampede to
return.

PETER

Will we see you later?

RIPLEY

I can't later.

PETER

And tomorrow?

RIPLEY

Tomorrow's possible. Do you know
Dinelli's? Piazza di Spagna?

PETER

I know the Piazza di Spagna. What time?

RIPLEY

Ten thirty?

PETER

We'll be there.

RIPLEY

Okay. Marge, see you tomorrow.
(to Peter)
It's really good to meet you.

INT. BOX, OPERA HOUSE. NIGHT.

Ripley goes straight to Meredith and grabs her.

> RIPLEY
>
> Let's go.

> MEREDITH
>
> I thought you were enjoying yourself?

> RIPLEY
>
> Let's take a carozza and look at the moon.

> MEREDITH
>
> You're crazy! It's freezing out there.

He's looking past her, where a mirror reflects Marge wading through the audience, Peter's elegant head getting danger-ously near as they approach their seats.

> RIPLEY
>
> C'mon, I need to talk to you. Just the two
> of us.

> MEREDITH
> *(quite taken)*
>
> Okay then, you're crazy.

EXT. CAROZZA, ROME. NIGHT.

Meredith shivers in the raw night as they cross the Tiber. Ripley as Dickie is confessing his heart belongs to Marge.

> MEREDITH
>
> Don't worry. Really. Don't worry.

> RIPLEY
>
> You're such a pal to understand. It's as if
> Marge is here now—I look at you and I see
> her face—and I can't, whatever I'm feeling
> towards you—I just can't...

MEREDITH
No, I absolutely understand. Of course.

RIPLEY
Otherwise you'd be fighting me off.

MEREDITH
Beating you away.

RIPLEY
I'm going to get out of Rome. I can just see
myself dragging you into my mess and it's
not fair.

MEREDITH
I think you should marry Marge.

RIPLEY
(kisses her hands)
You're a good person.

MEREDITH
You're a good person, Dickie. You're not a
rat.

EXT. MEREDITH'S APARTMENT, ROME.

They arrive at the courtyard outside Meredith's Apartment
Building. Ripley jumps down, collects her. She makes to go
inside, then looks at him.

MEREDITH
Will you meet me tomorrow? Just to say
good-bye in the daylight, properly? So it's
not just this, it's too…you should always
save pain for daylight…

RIPLEY
Oh Meredith, I'm sorry. Of course I'll meet
you. Let's have coffee in the morning at
Dinelli's.

                    M E R E D I T H
                      (fluttering)
I don't—is that by the Spanish Steps?

                      R I P L E Y
Exactly. Ten thirty—
              (instantly correcting himself)
Ten fifteen.

He gets back into the carozza. It moves off.

**EXT. DINELLI'S CAFÉ, PIAZZA DI SPAGNA.
MORNING.**

Meredith sits waiting in a café at the bottom of the Spanish
Steps. **Ripley, dressed as Ripley, is at the top of the steps,
among early tourists, watching as** she drinks her coffee at
an outside table. Then Marge and Peter appear walking up
the Via Condotti, head for another table, don't see Meredith.
She acknowledges Peter, who hasn't noticed her.

                    M E R E D I T H
Peter? Hello, it's Meredith Logue.

                      P E T E R
Of course it is, Meredith, hello, I'm sorry,
half-asleep, how are you? This is Marge
Sherwood. Meredith Logue.

                      M A R G E
Hello.

Hearing Marge's name Meredith reacts, freezes.

                      P E T E R
Join us, won't you? We're just waiting for a
friend. Do you know, I wonder did we see
you at the opera last night?

                    M E R E D I T H
I won't actually, although I think this might—
are you waiting for Dickie?

— 75 —

PETER

Well no, as it happens, although…

MARGE
(stunned at the mention of his name)

Dickie? Do you know Dickie?

MEREDITH

You were at the opera? Well, that explains—
yes I was there. I was there with Dickie.

MARGE
(to Peter)

I told you! I knew it!

MEREDITH
(getting up)

Marge, I don't know you, so I have no right,
but Dickie loves you. He's—I think you'll
find he's coming home to you.

MARGE
(proprietorial)

How would you know that?

MEREDITH

He told me everything. I was supposed to
meet him fifteen minutes ago, so I…I'm
going to go now, I think. Unless he meant *us*
to meet—which would be a little cruel,
wouldn't it?

PETER

No, we're meeting another friend. Tom
Ripley.

MARGE

Do you know Tom?

MEREDITH

Ripley? No. I heard about him, of course,
but no, I didn't meet him.

The WAITER has arrived to take orders. Meredith indicates she's leaving.

> MEREDITH (CONT'D)
>
> Not for me. No, *grazie.*

Marge is on the edge. Peter lays a hand to comfort her.

> MEREDITH (CONT'D)
>
> I hope I didn't complicate matters, but noth-
> ing, nothing untoward happened, nothing to
> prevent you from welcoming him back, from
> marrying him…Good-bye. Good-bye Peter,
> please don't get up.

Peter gets up. Ripley, from his vantage point at the top of the steps, watches Meredith leave and walk off into the crowd. He begins the slow walk down towards the square. As he becomes visible to the café, he starts to hurry. He's apologizing to Marge and Peter as they see him, in his element, lying and believing in his lie.

> RIPLEY
>
> Sorry, sorry. Had to renew my papers. Italian
> bureaucracy—never one stamp when they
> can make you line up for three. Have you
> been waiting long?

> PETER
>
> Not at all. Morning, Tom.

> RIPLEY
>
> Hi.
>
> *(to Marge)*
>
> Sorry. You okay? You look as if you've seen a
> ghost…

> MARGE
>
> Dickie was at the opera last night.

RIPLEY

I don't believe it. Wild horses wouldn't drag
Dickie to—

MARGE

He was there with someone. So I suppose
she must have dragged him—that's not fair.
I'm going back to Mongi. I think Dickie's
coming home.
                    (to Peter)
I'm going to go home.

RIPLEY

Really? That's swell. No, I was just—you're
way ahead of me! Great!

PETER

We think he's had a change of heart.
                    (to Marge)
So we should be celebrating.

MARGE

I hope so.

RIPLEY

It's fantastic. No, I was here last week at the
same time and bumped into Dickie coming
out of the American Express Office over
there. He was alone, by the way. It was, I'm
late now, I thought we might have seen him.
That's all. That was my news…
                    (to Peter)
I feel guilty. Marge doesn't understand this,
but anytime Dickie does something I feel
guilty.

EXT. ROME STREETS. AFTERNOON.

Ripley, on a SCOOTER, loaded with parcels, rides through
streets livened with Christmas decorations. He passes his

new landlady, Signora Buffi, at the entrance to his apartment building.

INT. STAIRS, PALAZZO GIOIA. DAY.

Ripley is being shown an APARTMENT FOR RENT in the Palazzo Gioia by a dry-witted older woman, SIGNORA BUFFI. They climb the many stairs. They speak in Italian.

> RIPLEY
>
> *C'e un* uh elevator uh—*ascensore nel palazzo?*
> (Is there an elevator in the building?)

> SIGNORA BUFFI
>
> *C'e giustizia al mondo?*
> (Is there justice in this world?)

INT. APARTMENT, PALAZZO GIOIA. DAY.

Ripley explores, relishing the decor. Signori Buffi fiddles and prods.

> SIGNORI BUFFI
>
> *Accendo il riscaldamento.*
> (I'll turn the heating on.)

> RIPLEY
> *(mimes playing sax)*
>
> *Mi piace suonare.*
> (I like to play music.)

> SIGNORI BUFFI
> *(shrugs)*
>
> *Io sono sorda. Quelli di sotto, una coppia,*
> *sono sordi. Allora, ti piace?*
> (I'm deaf. The couple below are deaf. So, do you like it?)

INT. RIPLEY'S APARTMENT. LATE AFTERNOON.

Ripley plunges into Bach's Italian Concerto on his new and

precious toy, a STEINWAY GRAND. His doorbell rings. He stops playing. He doesn't get visitors. He rises, a little nervous.

> RIPLEY

Hello?

> FREDDIE (O/S)

Dickie?

> RIPLEY

Who is it?

> FREDDIE (O/S)

It's Freddie. Let me in.

RIPLEY ALMOST COLLAPSES. He's faint.

> FREDDIE (O/S)

Dickie, come on, it's me.

Ripley can't think what to hide, where to hide. He opens the door.

> RIPLEY

Hello, Freddie, it's Tom, Tom Ripley.

> FREDDIE
> (confused, not pleasantly)

Oh hello, where's Dickie? How are you?

> RIPLEY

Yes, I'm good, thank you. Dickie's at dinner. He's at Otello's. Do you know it?

> FREDDIE

I don't think he's at dinner at six thirty P.M. If you said he was still at lunch I'd believe you. Incredible. The guy has disappeared off the face of the earth.

> RIPLEY

I guess.

FREDDIE

The landlady—as far as I could tell, the landlady said he was here right now.

RIPLEY

He's gone to dinner! Search the place. I can't
think why you would imagine Dickie would
hide from you.

FREDDIE

Because he's *been* hiding from me—what
happened at Christmas?

RIPLEY

What about Christmas?

FREDDIE

He was supposed to come skiing. I didn't get
a cable or a call or a note or, frankly, a fart.

Ripley has his hands behind his back. HE'S TUGGING
FRANTICALLY AT DICKIE'S RINGS. Ripley wanders into the
kitchen, turns on the tap to sluice his fingers.

RIPLEY (O/S)

Of course, he's been very involved in his
music, hasn't he? I think his theory is, you
know, you have to go into a cocoon before
you can become a butterfly.

FREDDIE

Which is horseshit. Have you heard him
play that thing?
(gesturing at the sax on its stand)
He can't.

RIPLEY (O/S)
(casually)
How did you find him? It's such an out of
the way apartment. Can I fix you a drink?

— 81 —

FREDDIE

No thanks.
(explaining his detective work)
Some kid at the American Express office.
(he starts to explore)
Are you living here?

Now he starts to hammer a nasty boogie-woogie on the piano.

RIPLEY
(returning, flinching)

No. No, I'm staying here for a few days, in Rome. That's a new piano, so you prob-

FREDDIE (O/S)

Did this place come furnished? It doesn't look like Dickie. Horrible isn't it?—so bourgeois.

Now he's poking at the Hadrian bust.

RIPLEY

You should watch that!

FREDDIE

In fact the only thing which look likes Dickie is you.

RIPLEY

Hardly.

FREDDIE

Have you done something to your hair?

Ripley starts to smile, his eyes darting around the room.

RIPLEY

Freddie, do you have something to say?

FREDDIE

What? I think I'm saying it. Something's going on. He's either converted to Christianity—or to something else.

I suggest you ask Dickie that yourself.
Otello's is on delle Croce, just off the Corso.

FREDDIE

Is it on *"delle Croce, just off the Corso"*?
You're a quick study, aren't you? Last time
you didn't know your ass from your elbow,
now you're giving me directions. That's not
fair, you probably do know your ass from
your elbow. I'll see you.

AND HE'S GONE. Ripley shuts the door, smooths the silk runner on the table where Freddie's hand had rucked it. He goes back to the door, opens it and looks over the rail.

INT. LANDING AND STAIRS, RIPLEY'S BUILD-ING. LATE DAY.

FREDDIE IS BACK IN CONVERSATION WITH SIGNORA BUFFI. Ripley can't make out the text but there's some discussion about *Signor Greenleaf* and *Signor Ripley*. Ripley hurries inside as Freddie's heavy shoes start to clump up the stairs again.

INT. RIPLEY'S APARTMENT. ROME. LATE DAY.

Freddie knocks on the door which pushes open. As he marches in, he launches into his interrogation.

FREDDIE

Ripley? There's someth-

—AND WALKS STRAIGHT INTO THE HEAD OF HADRIAN WHICH RIPLEY SWINGS AT HIM, AWKWARDLY HOLDING ON TO THE HEAVY MARBLE SCULPTURE WITH BOTH HANDS.

Freddie falls like an ox, first to his knees, groaning, then to the floor as Ripley brings the head down again, beating him downwards. As Freddie slumps away, Ripley loses his balance and the head sends Freddie a glancing blow before slipping from Ripley's grasp and smashing on to the floor. THE NOSE IS CHIPPED OFF.

EXT. PALAZZO GIOIA. NIGHT.

It's deserted. Ripley hauls Freddie out of the shadows towards the car. A couple walk across the square. Ripley talks to Freddie, berating him for his drunken stupor. He pushes him over the door and into the passenger seat.

> RIPLEY
> *(mimicking Freddie's voice)*
> Hey, if I'm drunk, think what her husband's saying.

EXT. VIA APPIA ANTICA. NIGHT.

The Fiat noses along THE APPIAN WAY. Black fragments of tombs punctuate either side of the poorly lit road. Inside the car, Ripley looks to left and right for a place to dump the body. He slows near a clump of trees.

INT. RIPLEY'S APARTMENT, ROME. EVENING.

Someone is KNOCKING urgently at the door. Ripley opens it, finds himself face to face with Signora Buffi and TWO POLICEMEN. One of them offers his hand.

> ROVERINI
> Dickie Greenleaf?

> RIPLEY
> Yes?

> ROVERINI
> Inspector Roverini. Can we come in?

INT. RIPLEY'S APARTMENT. EVENING.

Ripley sits with his head in his hands at the table. Roverini and his sergeant, BAGGIO, watch patiently.

RIPLEY

Poor Freddie, Jesus.

ROVERINI

Si. Si. It's a terrible shock, eh? What time did Signor Miles leave yesterday?

RIPLEY

I can't be absolutely sure—eight? nine? We'd both taken on far too many drinks—but it was dark, it was certainly dark when I walked him down to his car.

ROVERINI

So Signor Miles drove away and you did what?

RIPLEY

I went to bed. Freddie's a big man, but I'm in trouble after a couple of drinks. I've suffered all day. Who found him?

Roverini has walked over to the saxophone.

ROVERINI

Incidentally, could we ask you to identify the body?

RIPLEY

I'm sure Freddie had closer friends in Rome.
(*of the saxophone*)
You play?

ROVERINI

No. I like to listen. Alto. So, the Doctor, he
has to make the—
(looks at Baggio)
—come si dice?

RIPLEY

Postmortem?

ROVERINI

Yes, exactly, but his first, his first conclusion
was that Signor Miles was killed not later
than seven o'clock yesterday evening.

RIPLEY

Well, he certainly wasn't dead when he drove
off in his car.

ROVERINI

No.

RIPLEY

No.

EXT. AMERICAN EXPRESS, PIAZZA DI SPAGNA.
DAY.

Ripley emerges from the American Express Office. He has
the scooter. He slips Dickie's bag into his knapsack and rides
off.

EXT. NARROW STREET, THE GHETTO, ROME.
MORNING.

Ripley comes through a dark funnel in the Ghetto on his
scooter. He drives past a furniture store, DRESSING TABLES
AND MIRRORS spilling out onto the street. He glances side-
ways, sees his reflection fractured into several images and, for
an instant, it seems to him AS IF DICKIE'S THERE WATCH-
ING HIM. Ripley screams and swerves, crashing into the

pavement, the scooter falling onto him and pulling him along the cobbled passage. The man he thought to be Dickie, an Italian, runs up concerned.

EXT. SQUARE OF THE PALAZZO GIOIA. AFTERNOON.

Ripley drives towards the entrance. As Ripley gets off and pushes his scooter through the doorway SOME JOURNAL-ISTS, LOITERING INSIDE A BARBERSHOP, come running out and swarm around him with questions about Freddie. One of them gets off a photograph. It's chaos, a Police Officer shouts him away as Ripley puts up a protective hand and runs inside.

INT. ENTRANCE AND STAIRS, PALAZZO GIOIA. CONTINUOUS.

As Ripley hurries inside he encounters officers conducting more thorough forensic investigations in the stairwell. On a landing is Roverini. Ripley hurries towards him.

> RIPLEY
> Can we go up? Do you mind?

> ROVERINI
> Of course. What happened to your face?

> RIPLEY
> My scooter. I fell off. Getting chased by pho-
> tographers.

He hurries up the stairs, Roverini in tow.

> RIPLEY
> (agitated)
> The telephone, the press, I've been, I'm feel-
> ing hounded—do you think you could not
> give out my address?

                    ROVERINI

Never. We've had many requests and, of
course, we say no—even to your fiancée.

                    RIPLEY

I really don't want to see anybody.

                    ROVERINI

Even your fiancée…?

                    RIPLEY

Even her.

                    ROVERINI

What about Thomas Ripley?

                    RIPLEY

What about Ripley?

Ripley's way ahead and has reached the door of his apartment. He waits nervously for Roverini. He unlocks the door
and can barely wait for Roverini to catch up.

INT. RIPLEY'S APARTMENT. AFTERNOON.

Roverini follows Ripley inside.

                    ROVERINI

You and Signor Ripley went to San Remo, is
that right?

Ripley is appalled. He smiles.

                    RIPLEY

Yes, sure, we did go to San Remo. That was
months ago.

                    ROVERINI

November, I thought.

                    RIPLEY

Was it? Did you speak to Tom?

ROVERINI

November seventh is my information.

RIPLEY

I don't remember the exact date.

ROVERINI

And when did you last see Signor Ripley?

RIPLEY

A few days ago.

ROVERINI

Does he stay with you here?

RIPLEY

No!

ROVERINI

No. Here is a pattern. Two days ago Freddie
Miles is dead—he leaves your apartment and
is murdered. Yesterday a little boat is found
in San Remo full of rocks, and the owner
tells the police it was stolen on November
seventh. We look at hotel records and we see
oh! Dickie Greenleaf is staying in San Remo
and then our boatman remembers two
Americans taking a boat.

RIPLEY

It's not a pattern, it's a coincidence. There
must be fifty hotels in San Remo, there must
have been a hundred people renting a boat
on that day.

ROVERINI

Thirty-one people.

RIPLEY

Thirty-one people. What are we supposed to
have done in the boat?

Baggio appears. Speaks to Roverini. Ripley is getting cranky.

ROVERINI

That is Miss Sherwood now. Marge
Sherwood.

RIPLEY
(appalled, defeated)

Let her in, what's the difference? Let her in.
(Baggio is on his way to the door.)
No, actually, no, I'd like it very much if you
would ask her to come back later.

Roverini nods, mutters to Baggio, who heads out.

RIPLEY

Thank you.

ROVERINI
(watching him)

May I ask…why would you speak to your
friend and not your fiancée?

RIPLEY

I think I just said. Ripley was handling some
business for me, nor does Mr. Ripley want to
marry me. Nor did he ask me every day if I
would marry him. And when.

ROVERINI

Do you have a photograph of Signor Ripley?

RIPLEY

I'm not in the habit of carrying around photographs of my male friends.

ROVERINI

Now I think I have upset you. My English
perhaps is coarse.

RIPLEY

It is a little coarse, yes.

ROVERINI

Sorry. No one has seen Signor Ripley since
San—

RIPLEY

I have!

ROVERINI

You have, yes.

RIPLEY

No, I have and so has Miss Sherwood, ask
her! and if I could remember which hotel he
was staying at—*the Goldoni!*—Tom was staying at the Goldoni.

ROVERINI

Good. The Goldoni. Yes—you're right. A
coincidence.
(he gets up to leave)
I look forward to our next meeting when I
will be more careful with my English and
persuade you to play me your saxophone.
Alto.

RIPLEY

Absolutely.

ROVERINI
(suddenly turning)
I have a witness who thinks they saw two
men getting into Mr. Miles' car. That
couldn't have been you?

RIPLEY
(thrown, scrabbling)

Well, I don't drive. I can't drive a car. I even
seem to be having trouble managing a scooter, so no, it wasn't me.

ROVERINI
(ominously)

Did I say you were driving? I don't think I
did.

Ripley lets them out, heaves a heavy sigh, then opens the
door again, looks down to see Roverini speaking to Marge on
the stairs. Marge looks up, Ripley shuts the door, the noose
tightening. He leans against the door, then suddenly a voice
shocks him upright.

MARGE

Dick? Dickie? I know you can hear me.
What am I doing, chasing you around…? I
was going to say I would count to three and
if you didn't open the door, but I won't
count anymore. On you. I won't count on
you anymore. Whatever it is, whatever you've
done or haven't done, you've broken my
heart. That's one thing I know you're guilty
of, and I don't know why, I don't know why,
I just don't know why…

Ripley listens, there's a silence, then Marge's footsteps as
they ring out on the stone stairs. The tapping sound resolves
into the tap-tap of a manual typewriter.

**INT. RIPLEY'S APARTMENT, PALAZZO GIOIA.
NIGHT.**

Ripley's AT THE TYPEWRITER, HE BEGINS TO TYPE.

*Rome, January 6, 1959. My dear Tom, I'm
getting out of this. Freddie's death, Silvana...*

INT. RIPLEY'S APARTMENT, PALAZZO GIOIA. NIGHT.

CHAOS. Ripley is working quickly, selecting clothes, dividing them into TWO PILES—one for Dickie's trunk, one for his own battered suitcase. He puts the license plates from Freddie's car in Dickie's luggage. He has placed one shirt on the Ripley pile then checks again, and, on seeing Dickie's initials, places it with the bigger pile, then picks it up again and holds it briefly to his cheek. He takes Dickie's rings, opens up a LITTLE BOX of buttons and needles and cuff links and sadly tosses them in. Dickie's leather writing case goes on the big pile, too, as do cuff links, ties, the Mont Blanc, Dickie's passport, which he opens to **scratch at the photograph**, obliterating the face.

> ### RIPLEY (O/S)
> *...I've thought about going to the police, but I
> can't do it, I can't face it. I can't face any-
> thing anymore. I wish I could give you the life
> I took for granted. You'd make better use of
> what I've had and wasted. I don't think my
> parents even like me very much. I think they
> have an idea of a son and they don't care for
> my version of him. In all kinds of ways you're
> much more the kind of son my father wanted.
> I've made a mess of being Dickie Greenleaf,
> haven't I?...*

He's finished the letter, signs it, puts it in an envelope marked **Tom Ripley** and places the letter on top of the piano next to Dickie's passport. His head is reflected in the distorting curve of the lid. As he puts on his glasses there's a moment when there are two heads slowly separating, as Ripley leaves behind his brief life as Dickie Greenleaf.

INT. BASEMENT, PALAZZO GIOIA. NIGHT.

Ripley carries Dickie's luggage down into THE COMMUNAL BASEMENT of the Gioia, a wretched place full of shadows and gloom and the overflow from thirty apartments. A red plush couch sits on top of a mound of furniture. He finds some dust sheets and shoves the cases under them. Then Dickie's saxophone.

> RIPLEY (O/S)
> *...Now I can't think what to do, or where to go. I'm haunted by everything I've done, and can't undo. I realize you can change the people, change the scenery, but you can't change your own rotten self...*

Outside the small window, Ripley sees uniformed feet and the revolving blue light of a Police Car. He shrinks back, turns off the light, and disappears into the dark, illuminated fitfully by the strobe of cold blue.

EXT. BY THE PALAZZO GIOIA, ROME. NIGHT.

Ripley, familiar battered luggage in tow, appears at the entrance of the building next to his own, glances at the police car parked opposite the big doors, then hurries off into the darkness.

> RIPLEY (O/S)
> *...Maybe this is the easy way out, but then...*

EXT. BY THE PALAZZO GIOIA. NIGHT.

Ripley's briefly silhouetted as he scuttles down an alley, hurrying towards a gate, and disappears behind it.

R I P L E Y (O/S)

...that's yours truly all over—isn't it?...

INT. TRAIN FROM ROME. BEFORE DAWN.

It's raining. Ripley's asleep on the train. It jolts suddenly and rouses him.

R I P L E Y (O/S)

...You've always understood what's at the heart of me, Tom. Marge never could. I sup-pose that's why I'm writing this to you, the brother I never had, the only true friend I ever had. I'm sorry.

In the window's reflection he sees his own face, moves his head, but can't any longer summon Dickie.

EXT. FIELD, TOSCANA. DAWN.

Ripley emerges from a tent, which sits on a hill overlooking the renaissance valleys of Tuscany. In the distance a small hill town. It's freezing, flakes of snow drift in the chill wind. He shakes out his sleeping bag. He jogs with the cold.

EXT. TUSCAN PIAZZA. DAY.

Ripley, unshaven, walks towards a newspaper stand. A couple of ITALIAN NEWSPAPERS have lurid front page stories about Dickie's disappearance. They're running the shot from the Palazzo Gioia—a blurred photograph, Ripley's hand raised, a policeman half-blocking him.

INT. CAFE, TUSCAN PIAZZA. DAY.

Ripley is inside a café, making a phone call. Outside in the square, a small windswept wedding party emerges from the church, the bride evidently in some spat with her husband. Ripley has some of the newspapers folded on the shelf. He's dialing a number from a card with Peter's name on it.

> RIPLEY
>
> Peter? It's Tom, Tom Ripley. I'm in Tuscany, I've just seen the newspapers…I know…I had no idea…

EXT. PIAZZALE ROMA, VENICE. DAWN.

Ripley sits next to his battered luggage at the prow of a MOTOR TAXI as it surges towards Venice at dawn.

> RIPLEY (O/S)
>
> *No, I haven't seen him… That's why I was calling…I need your help with that…Really?…I've always wanted to see Venice.*

Peter Smith-Kingsley waits on the quay. Ripley waves. Peter waves back.

> PETER
> *(indicating the taxi stop)*
> I'll see you over there!

EXT. ST. MARK'S SQUARE, VENICE. EARLY MORNING.

Ripley and Peter walk through the square, the pigeons scattering. Ripley breathes in the atmosphere, the beautiful grey.

> RIPLEY
>
> Peter, I'm really sorry to put you through this. I just couldn't face going to the police by myself when my Italian's so rotten.

> PETER
>
> Don't be daft. It's fine. I'm delighted you finally made it to Venice. I'm delighted, contrary to rumor, you're still in one piece.

RIPLEY

What rumor?

PETER

That Dickie murdered you and is traveling
under your passport. I know, ridiculous.

INT. POLICE STATION, VENICE. LATE DAY.

Later. Ripley sits in the middle of a bustling Police Station,
where thefts, tourists, thieves and complaints are being
processed. The station is in an old brewery or armory. It's a
horrible, monochrome, oppressive place. Peter is in conversation at a desk, turns and walks over to where Ripley waits.

PETER

Welcome to Venice. This place reeks,
doesn't it? Can you smell it? Ugh. Sorry.
Not the best way to spend your first day.

RIPLEY

It's okay.

PETER

Anyway I've got to the bottom of the delay.
Finally. We're waiting for someone from
Rome.

RIPLEY
(completely thrown)

What do you mean? They're sending someone from Rome?

PETER

That's good, isn't it?

RIPLEY
(as if suffocating)

No, but I thought that didn't happen in Italy,
that each region was completely separate! I
was *sure* that was the—

PETER

You've seen the papers, you know what a big
deal it's been here. American tourist murdered—

RIPLEY

It's ridiculous but now you've mentioned the
stench I can hardly breathe.

A door opens. COLONEL VERRECCHIA, fresh from Rome,
and a sullen wedge of a man, comes in, scowling at the couple. Ripley dares not look up in case it's Roverini. A
POLICEMAN introduces him.

POLICEMAN

Colonelo Verrecchia della Polizia di Roma.

VERRECCHIA
(to Peter, in Italian)

Qui e Ripley? Who is Ripley?

PETER
(in Italian)

Lui. Him.

VERRECCHIA

E lei? And you?

PETER

Sono un amico—traduco per lui. I'm a friend,
translating for him.

Verrecchia strides past them and into a smaller, interview
room at the back of the station. His manner is ominous.

INT. POLICE STATION, INTERVIEW ROOM.
VENICE. LATE DAY.

This room is not at all friendly. There is evidence of a locked
area for cells at one wall. A small, sour window gives onto a

canal. The main station is glimpsed through some internal windows. Peter and Ripley come through. Verrecchia sits down. Verrecchia talks in staccato Italian, during which Peter translates.

> **VERRECCHIA**
>
> *Ho assunto io la guida delle indagini in seguito alla negativa valutazione delle disdicevoli circostanze verificatesi con il mio predecessore Roverini che come e noto non e riuscito a impedire il verificarsi della scomparsa del signor Greenleaf, il quale era l'unica persona al momento passibile di incriminazione del reato di omicidio del signor Miles.*

> **PETER**
> *(translating)*
>
> He's taken over the case because... they're annoyed the previous chap let Dickie...disappear when he was the only, he was the only suspect in Freddie's murder.

> **VERRECCHIA**
>
> *Quando e stata l'ultima volta che il signor Ripley ha visto il signor Greenleaf?*
> When was the last time Ripley saw Greenleaf?

Ripley forgets he's not supposed to have much Italian and answers.

> **RIPLEY**
>
> In Rome, about three weeks ago.
> *(shrugs)*
> I knew that one.

> **PETER**
> *(giving Ripley a look)*
> *A Roma, circa tre settimane fa.*

VERRECCHIA

Dove e stato il signor Ripley da allora?

PETER
(translating)

Where have you been since then?

RIPLEY

I've been backpacking.

PETER

I don't know how to translate that.
(he tries)
*E difficile...il signor Ripley...dormiva
all'aperto, con un...*

VERRECCHIA

All'aperto? Col freddo che ha fatto?

PETER

He thinks it's very cold to be sleeping outside.

VERRECCHIA

*Il signor Ripley ha sviluppate tendenze
omosessuali?*

PETER

Are you a homosexual?
(then as himself)
Interesting non sequitur.

RIPLEY

No.

PETER
(translates for him)

No.
(as Peter, drily)
By the way, officially there are no Italian
homosexuals. Makes Leonardo,
Michelangelo very inconvenient.

RIPLEY

Tell him I have a fiancée, Dickie has a
fiancée, and Freddie Miles probably had a
string of them.

PETER
(translating)

*Il signor Ripley ha una fidanzata, il signor
Dickie ha una fidanzata e probabilmente il
signor Freddie Miles ha molte fidanzate.*

VERRECCHIA
(laughs)

Mamma mia, quante fidanzate!

They all laugh.

RIPLEY

What did he say?

PETER

He says so many fiancées.

VERRECCHIA
(suddenly very tough)

*Lei ha ucciso prima Freddie Miles e dopo
Dickie Greenleaf! Vero?*

As Peter translates Verrecchia watches intently.

PETER

He wants to know if you killed Freddie Miles
and then killed Dickie Greenleaf?

RIPLEY
(outraged)

No I did not. I did not kill Freddie Miles and
then kill Dickie Greenleaf. Is he accusing
me?
(Peter clearly doesn't ask)
Ask him if he's accusing me!

PETER

He's already angry, I don't think—

RIPLEY
(interrupting, heated)

Just because he doesn't like Americans!

VERRECCHIA

*Non e questo il luogo per le vostre
conversazioni private!* (This is not the
place for your private conversations.)

PETER
(appeasing him)

A ragione. A ragione. (You're right. You're
right.)

VERRECCHIA

Hmm. C'e questa… (There's this…)

Verrecchia hands over a letter. It's opened. Ripley's name on
the outside. Ripley stares at it.

VERRECCHIA (CONT'D)

*Questa lettera e stata trovata nell'abitazione
del signor Richard Greenleaf a Roma.*

PETER

They found this in Dickie's place in Rome.

RIPLEY

You opened this?

VERRECCHIA

Of course!

RIPLEY
(pointing at the envelope)

This is my name!

He stands and takes the letter out. Begins to read. He has
the look of a man whose privacy has been violated.

RIPLEY (CONT'D)
(to Peter)
It's a suicide note.
(to Verrecchia)
You ask me all these questions and you've
already read this suicide note?

EXT. VIALE SAN SPIRIDONE, VENICE. DAY.

Ripley follows Peter Smith-Kingsley down a slit of an alley.

RIPLEY
This is swell of you, Peter.

PETER
Not at all. I'm going to be very popular with
the Contessa. No one's renting anything. And
if they won't let you leave Venice, which is
ridiculous, you may as well be comfortable.

They arrive at a Palazzo. Peter fiddles with keys.

PETER
I have to warn you—it's probably damp. And
camp. All Venetian Palazzi are of the damp
and camp variety.

INT. VENICE PALAZZO CANAL FLOOR. DAY.

He gets the door open. It leads into an unpromising, pud-
dled, dank and empty ground floor. He navigates to the other
end where there is another set of large doors.

PETER
In this case, very damp.

INT. PALAZZO. DAY.

The little Palazzo is magnificent, faded, chilly, slightly abandoned—the furnishings covered. Ripley loves it.

RIPLEY

It's wonderful.

PETER

It will be. Just needs a bit of sorting out.

He pulls open a shutter, raising a cloud of dust and revealing San Marco in all its glory across the Grand Canal.

PETER

Well, that is wonderful!

Ripley, overwhelmed, walks over and stands beside him.

PETER (CONT'D)

I don't believe that letter. Do you? Dickie's letter? Do you believe it?
(Ripley doesn't answer)
What do you see in him? Actually, why am I asking. We all fell for it. So easy to love, so hard to like.

RIPLEY

I thought you and Dickie were friends?

PETER

We are. I thought you and Dickie were lovers—
(looks at Ripley)
—according to Marge at least.

He walks back into the room, a little distracted.

RIPLEY
(noncommittal)

And the police.

PETER

Well, she'd have them arrest you for stealing Dickie away from her. As if anybody could make Dickie do anything. So stubborn and so dazzling, of course.

He's gone to the next window, opens that, too.

> **PETER**
> Well, will you take it?

Hearing what he thinks is a snort of enthusiasm, he turns round to find Ripley sitting in an armchair, still covered with its sheet, WEEPING UNCONTROLLABLY. Peter's mortified.

> **PETER**
> Oh Lord, I'm sorry.

Ripley shakes his head, the tears pouring, real tears, at the full realization of what he's done.

> **RIPLEY**
> I miss him, I miss him. He's dead. I miss
> him.

Peter stands by him, a consoling hand on his shoulder.

INT. PETER SMITH-KINGSLEY'S APARTMENT. DAY.

There's music everywhere—and stands—and posters of performances and PHOTOGRAPHS OF PETER CONDUCTING. Peter is an opera *repetiteur*. Ripley is sitting at Peter's piano, playing from the score of Vivaldi's *Stabat Mater*. Peter's made supper. He's setting the table.

> **PETER**
> Can you imagine, if Dickie did kill Freddie,
> what that must be like? To wake up every
> morning, how can you? Just wake up and be
> a person, drink a coffee...?

> **RIPLEY**
> Whatever you do, however terrible, however
> hurtful—it all makes sense, doesn't it? Inside

your head. You never meet anybody who thinks they're a bad person or that they're cruel.

PETER

But you're still tormented, you must be, you've killed somebody…

RIPLEY

Don't you put the past in a room, in the cellar, and lock the door and just never go in there? Because that's what I do.

PETER

Probably. In my case it's probably a whole building.

RIPLEY

Then you meet someone special and all you want to do is toss them the key, say *open up, step inside,* but you can't because it's dark and there are demons and if anybody saw how ugly it was…

Peter's come over, stands behind him over the piano.

PETER

That's the music talking. Harder to be bleak if you're playing *Knees up Mother Brown.*

He vamps this vaudeville song over Ripley's shoulder.

RIPLEY

I keep wanting to do that—fling open the door—let the light in, clean everything out. If I could get a huge eraser and rub everything out…starting with myself.

PETER

Don't touch your face. Misery-guts.

                    RIPLEY
That's the first thing I'd rub out…

                    PETER
No really. Don't.

                    RIPLEY
Actually, the second.

                    PETER
What's the first?
                (no answer from Ripley)
No key, huh?

Peter starts to play again. Ripley looks at him, smiles, joins in.

EXT. VENICE S.LUCIA. RAILWAY STATION. DAY.

MARGE appears on the steps, carrying an overnight bag. Ripley and Peter have come to meet her.

                    MARGE
                (kissing him warmly)
Hello Peter, so good to see you.

                    RIPLEY
Hello Marge!

                    MARGE
                (kissing Ripley cooly)
Tom.

They walk towards the Vaporetto.

                MARGE (CONT'D)
So you found Peter…

                    PETER
I think we sort of found each other.

Marge smiles enigmatically. Ripley registers.

PETER

Where's Dickie's father?

MARGE

He's not coming till the morning. Evidently
his stomach—I don't think the food here is
agreeing with him.

RIPLEY

I was looking forward to seeing him.

MARGE

Dickie hasn't killed himself. I'm sure of that.
There's a private detective on the case now—
a Mr. MacCarron—Dickie's father's employ-
ing him.

RIPLEY

That's a terrific idea.

MARGE

He's American. He's already discovered
Dickie cashed checks for a thousand dollars
the day before he disappeared.

They step onto the Vaporetto.

MARGE

Is that what you do before you jump in the
Tiber? I don't think so.

EXT. RIPLEY HOUSE, VENICE. DAY.

The boat arrives at the entrance to the house. Peter opens the
door as Ripley collects Marge's bags.

MARGE
(to Peter)

Is this you?

PETER

No, it's Tom's. Splendid, eh?

MARGE

Golly. Who's paying for this?

RIPLEY

Peter found it for me. I can afford it because
it's damp and, and falling down.

INT. RIPLEY'S HOUSE, VENICE. DAY.

Marge, entering the living room, is astonished at its grandeur.
She walks around as Ripley heads for the bar.

MARGE

This is spectacular.

PETER

That's why Tom wanted you to stay. It's better than squeezing into my room, and I know
how you hate hotels.

MARGE

A hotel would have been fine.
(to Ripley)
We'll have to tell Mr. Greenleaf how far his
dollar has stretched.

Ripley is shaking a martini. Marge laughs, helpless, somehow
raging. Peter turns.

PETER

What's funny?

MARGE

No, nothing. I'm just thinking about when
Tom arrived in Mongi.
(to Ripley)
And now look at you.

RIPLEY

Look at me what?

MARGE

To the manner born.

EXT. PIAZZA SAN MARCO, VENICE. DAY.

St. Mark's Square is buzzing with life—tourists, balloon sell-
ers—a man playing saxophone. HERBERT GREENLEAF sits
out in the colonnade on one of the many tables at Florian's
Café, cradling a glass of hot water. He gets up as Marge and
Ripley arrive.

RIPLEY

Mr. Greenleaf.

HERBERT GREENLEAF

Tom, how are you? You look well.

RIPLEY

I'm well, thank you.

HERBERT GREENLEAF

Far cry from New York.

RIPLEY

Yes it is.

HERBERT GREENLEAF

Marge, good morning. Unusual weather.

RIPLEY

And you, sir? Any better?

HERBERT GREENLEAF

Pretty good. Sticking with hot water.

MARGE

Where's Mr. MacCarron?

HERBERT GREENLEAF

San Remo. The police are amateurs. Well,
my boy, it's come to a pretty pass, hasn't it?

RIPLEY

Yes. —What's the detective hoping to find in
San Remo?

HERBERT GREENLEAF

He's being thorough, that's all. I'm learning
about my son, Tom, now he's missing. I'm
learning a great deal about him. I hope you can
fill in some more blanks for me. Marge has been
good enough to do that, about Mongibello.

RIPLEY

I'll try my best, sir. Obviously I'll do anything to help Dickie.

Marge looks at him in contempt.

HERBERT GREENLEAF

This theory, the letter he left for you, the
police think that's a clear indication he was
planning on doing something...to himself.

MARGE

I just don't believe that!

HERBERT GREENLEAF

You don't want to, dear. Marge, what a man
may say to his sweetheart and what he'll
admit to another fellow—

MARGE

Such as?

HERBERT GREENLEAF

I'd like to talk to Tom alone—perhaps this
afternoon? Would you mind?

MARGE

Not at all. I'm going with Peter to explore the
Accademia.

HERBERT GREENLEAF
What a waste of lives and opportunities
and—

The saxophonist is blaring away in the piazza. Greenleaf
suddenly explodes.

HERBERT GREENLEAF (CONT'D)
—I'd pay that fellow a hundred dollars right
now to shut up!

INT. RIPLEY'S HOUSE. AFTERNOON.

Herbert Greenleaf sits on a chair, Ripley pours him some tea.

HERBERT GREENLEAF
(reading, plunging into gloom)
Why couldn't he write us about these things?
Why couldn't he telephone me before he did
something stupid?
(reads on, stung)
*"I've thought about going to the police. But I
can't face it. I can't face anything anymore."*
I see. No, Marge doesn't know the half of it.

RIPLEY
I think it might hurt her to know.

HERBERT GREENLEAF
And his passport photo? Can you imagine—
to scratch out your own face like that—the
frame of mind you'd have to be in?

RIPLEY
I feel guilty. I think I pushed him away from
me.

HERBERT GREENLEAF
(such a disappointed father)
Well, if we all pushed him away what about
him pushing us away? You've been a great

— 112 —

HERBERT GREENLEAF (CONT'D)

friend to my son. Everything is someone else's fault. Why is it wrong for a girl to want a man to make a commitment? We all have responsibilities—that's not pushy, that's common morality. Somebody's got to—what's the word?

(Ripley shakes his head)

The moment someone confronts him he lashes out. You know, people always say you can't choose your parents, but you can't choose your children.

INT. RIPLEY'S HOUSE, VENICE. DUSK.

Ripley wakes up from an awful, chilling nightmare, his head full of ghosts. He's cramped up in an armchair, his arms in some fetal protection. HIS DOOR KNOCKER IS BEING REPEATEDLY SHAKEN. He surfaces thickly, stumbles to the door. It's Peter and Marge.

RIPLEY

I'm sorry. I was asleep. I must have fallen asleep.

PETER

You look ghastly, Tom. Are you okay?

MARGE

Did Dickie's dad go?

RIPLEY

He's having an early night.

MARGE

Poor man.

(she heads to her room)

We were knocking on that door forever.

(she fiddles inside the sleeve of her dress)

I think I've broken my strap.

PETER

Not guilty.

RIPLEY

I'll fix some drinks.

MARGE

You *walk* in Venice!

She takes off her shoe, examining her feet for wear and tear, then disappears into the bedroom. Peter walks over to Ripley, a little concerned.

PETER

Are you okay?

RIPLEY

I'm fine.

PETER
(a hand on his shoulder)
Do you want me to stick around?

RIPLEY

It's okay.

PETER

Or I could come back.

Ripley looks at him. That's never happened. He digs in his pocket, finds his key, gives it to Peter. Peter smiles.

PETER (CONT'D)

Your key.

INT. RIPLEY'S BATHROOM, VENICE. NIGHT.
Ripley's in the bath. Marge knocks on his door.

MARGE (O/S)

Tom?

RIPLEY

Marge, I'm in the bath. Won't be long.

MARGE (O/S)

Tom, I need to talk to you. It's urgent.

Ripley, irritated, opens the door, his towel wrapped around his waist. Marge is white. She's wearing a robe. She's slightly breathless.

MARGE

I found Dickie's rings.

RIPLEY

What?

MARGE

You've got Dickie's rings.

RIPLEY

I can explain.

He can't. His eyes dart. Marge holds up the evidence.

MARGE

Dickie promised me he would never take off this ring.

RIPLEY

Let me put on some clothes and then we can talk about this.

MARGE

I have to tell Mr. Greenleaf. I have to tell Mr. Greenleaf. I have to tell Mr. Greenleaf.

RIPLEY

Marge, calm down, you're being hysterical.

MARGE

He promised me. *I swear I'll never take off this ring until the day—*

RIPLEY

Shut up! Shut up!

His towel slips off from his waist.

— 115 —

R I P L E Y (CONT'D)
I'm wet, Marge, I've lost my towel, I'd really
like to put my clothes on. So go and pour us
both a drink, will you?

She goes out obediently, a zombie. He shuts the door.
Immediately he starts looking for something, anything, to kill
Marge with. He's got a shoe but it feels too light. He opens
cabinets, drawers—nail scissors, nothing—then picks up his
straight razor and considers it in the mirror.

**INT. RIPLEY'S SITTING ROOM. VENICE.
NIGHT.**

Marge is leaving, coat on, as Ripley comes out of the bathroom.

R I P L E Y

Marge? Where are you going?

M A R G E
(like a creature caught in headlights)
I was looking for a needle and thread. I
wasn't snooping. I was looking for a needle
and thread to mend my bra.

R I P L E Y
The scent you're wearing. *I* bought it for
you, not Dickie. The thing about Dickie. So
many things. The day he was late back from
Rome— I tried to tell you this—he was with
another girl. I'm not talking about Meredith,
another girl we met in a bar. He couldn't be
faithful for five minutes. So when he makes a
promise it doesn't mean what it means when
you make a promise. Or I do. He has so
many realities, Dickie, and he believes them
all. He lies. He lies, that's his...half the time
he doesn't even realize.

A SMALL RED STAIN is appearing on the pocket of his robe. As he speaks the stain spreads. He looks at it absently.

> **R I P L E Y**
>
> Today, for the first time, I've even wondered whether he might have killed Freddie. He would get so crazy if anybody contradicted him—well, you know that. Marge. I loved you —you might as well know—I loved you, and because he knew I loved you, he let you think I loved him. Didn't you see, couldn't you see? I don't know, maybe it's grotesque to say this now, so just write it on a piece of paper or something, and keep it in your purse for a rainy day. *Tom loves me.*

> **M A R G E**
> *(as if she'd heard nothing)*
> Why do you have Dickie's rings?

His hand goes to his pocket. HE'S GOING TO HAVE TO DO IT.

> **R I P L E Y**
> I told you. He gave them to me.

> **M A R G E**
> Why? When?

> **R I P L E Y**
> I feel as if you haven't heard anything I've been saying to you.

> **M A R G E**
> I don't believe you.

> **R I P L E Y**
> It's all true.

> **M A R G E**
> I don't believe a single word you've said.

Marge is shivering. Ripley, ominous, advances, she retreats.

RIPLEY
You're shivering, Marge. Can I hold you?
Would you let me hold you?

Marge panics, backed up against the door. She screams and
turns straight into the arms of a startled PETER who's come
back to visit Ripley, and is unlocking the door.

MARGE
(sobbing uncontrollably)
Oh Peter!

Ripley storms off. His hand comes out of his pocket COV-
ERED IN BLOOD from the razor. Peter notices, appalled.

RIPLEY
(to Peter)
You try. You try talking to her.

PETER
(calls after him)
Tom. Tom! Tell me, what's going on?

RIPLEY
(not turning round)
I give up.

INT. RIPLEY HOUSE, LIVING ROOM. NIGHT.

Peter has just put a Band-Aid over Ripley's cut hand.

PETER
You can't be angry with her. She's upset and
needs someone to blame. So she blames you.
I'll talk to her. As for you—either get a safety
razor or grow a beard.

He takes a hot drink and a hot water bottle next door for
Marge. Ripley stays behind, moves to where he can see
through the slit of the door's hinge as Peter takes care of her.

MARGE

Peter, I'm not staying here, whatever you say.
I'll go to a hotel if there's no room with you.
Just promise me you won't leave me alone
with him. Promise me.

PETER

Marge, of course you can stay with me, but
what has Tom done? It would be terrible, I
think, if through all this, when it's Dickie,
Dickie—you're blaming Tom for everything
Dickie's done to you.

**INT. LOBBY, EUROPA REGINA HOTEL, VENICE.
MORNING.**

Ripley hurries through the gleaming marble entrance.

**INT. HERBERT GREENLEAF SUITE, EUROPA
REGINA. DAY.**

Ripley knocks on the door. It's opened by a face he doesn't
recognize. A middle-aged heavyset man. It's MacCARRON,
the private investigator.

RIPLEY

Is Mr. Greenleaf here?

MACCARRON

Mr. Ripley? I'm Alvin MacCarron.

MARGE (O/S)

I don't know, I don't know, I just know it.

HERBERT GREENLEAF (O/S)

*Marge, there's female intuition, and then
there are facts—*

Greenleaf sits with a scrubbed Marge, her hair pulled back,
as if newly widowed. THE RINGS SIT GLINTING ON THE
COFFEE TABLE.

HERBERT GREENLEAF

Tom.

RIPLEY

Hello, sir.

(smiles thinly at Marge)

Marge, you should have waited, didn't Peter tell you I'd come by and pick you up?

HERBERT GREENLEAF

Marge has been telling us about the rings.

RIPLEY

You know I feel ridiculous I didn't mention them yesterday—I clean forgot—ridiculous.

HERBERT GREENLEAF

Perhaps you didn't mention them because there's only one conclusion to be drawn.

Ripley worries about what that conclusion is as Mr. Greenleaf heads into his bedroom.

HERBERT GREENLEAF

Mr. MacCarron did something the Roman police didn't bother to do. He searched the basement of the apartment building where my son was living. The rings were not the only things he left behind. He found this.

He returns from his bedroom with DICKIE'S SAXOPHONE CASE, opens it. The SAXOPHONE gleams.

HERBERT GREENLEAF

I can assure you that's not what my wife wants me to bring home with me. I'm going to take Marge for a little walk, Tom. Mr. MacCarron wants to talk with you.

> RIPLEY
> *(feeling caged in)*

We could go down to the bar—no need for
you to—

> HERBERT GREENLEAF

No, he should talk to you alone.

He helps Marge to her feet and leads her out. RIPLEY IS
PARALYZED. He waits for the door to shut. Aimlessly he
walks out onto the terrace, with its staggering, beautiful and
indifferent view.

EXT. EUROPA REGINA, THE GREENLEAF TERRACE. DAY.

Ripley stands, steels himself for MacCarron's charges.

> RIPLEY
>
> I could probably see my bedroom from here.
> I can see my house. When you see where you
> live from a distance it's like a dream, isn't it?

> MACCARRON
> *(coming out)*
>
> I don't care for B.S. I don't care to hear it. I
> don't care to speak it.

> RIPLEY

Okay.

> MACCARRON
>
> Why do you think Dickie's father sent him to
> Europe in the first place? Did you know at
> Princeton Dickie Greenleaf half-killed a boy?

Ripley turns, shocked.

> MACCARRON (CONT'D)
>
> At a party. Over some girl. He kicked the kid
> several times in the head. Put him in the hos-

> MACCARRON (CONT'D)
>
> pital. The boy had a wire fixed in his jaw.
> The Rome police didn't think to ask Mr.
> Greenleaf.

MacCarron gets up.

> MACCARRON (CONT'D)
>
> Nor did they think to check whether a
> Thomas Ripley had ever been a student at
> Princeton University. I turned up a Tom
> Ripley who'd been a piano tuner in the
> music department.

Ripley's head drops.

> MACCARRON (CONT'D)
>
> See—in America we're taught to check a fact
> before it becomes a fact. We're taught to nose
> around when a girl drowns herself, find out if
> that girl was pregnant, find out if Dickie had
> an embarrassment there.

Ripley doesn't know where this barrage is going.

> MACCARRON (CONT'D)
>
> Mr. Greenleaf appreciates your loyalty. He
> really does. Marge, she's got a hundred theo-
> ries, but there are a few things she doesn't
> know. We hope she never knows.

> RIPLEY
>
> I hope she never knows.

> MACCARRON
>
> Three different people saw Dickie get into
> Freddie Miles' car. A man who won't identify
> himself because he was jumping someone
> else's wife at the time saw Dickie removing
> license plates from a red sports car. The

MACCARRON (CONT'D)

police know about this man because he happens to be a policeman.

He walks out of the room, returns carrying THE LICENSE
PLATES from Freddie's car.

MACCARRON (CONT'D)

I found these in the basement of Dickie's
apartment. They belonged to Freddie's car.
Mr. Greenleaf has asked me to lose them in
the canal this evening.

Ripley can't believe what he's hearing. It's like a dream.

MACCARRON (CONT'D)

Mr. Greenleaf also feels there was a silent
promise in Dickie's letter to you which he
intends to honor. He intends to transfer a
good part of Dickie's income from his trust
into your name. He doesn't intend to give the
Italian police any information about Dickie's
past. He's rather hoping you'll feel the same.

There is a silence in which this strange compact is agreed.

RIPLEY

Do you have any American cigarettes?

EXT. EUROPA REGINA MOORING. DAY.

Ripley stands with Marge, Mr. Greenleaf and MacCarron at
the water's edge—MOTOR LAUNCH growling. They shake
hands, and then MacCarron and Mr. Greenleaf get into the
launch. Herbert Greenleaf carries the saxophone case.

RIPLEY
(to Marge)

I feel I never should have said those things to
you the other evening. I was pretty flustered,

the rings and—and you looked so, I don't
know.

Marge shakes her head to silence him.

RIPLEY

But I hope that note goes to New York in
your purse, for a rainy day.

MARGE

What are you going to do now, Tom?

RIPLEY

I don't know. Peter has a concert in Athens
next month—and he's asked if I want to go
along, help out. He says good-bye by the way
—he's in rehearsal, otherwise—

MARGE

Why do I think there's never been a Ripley
rainy day?

RIPLEY

What?

MARGE
(lunging at him)

**I know it was you—I know it was you,
Tom. I know it was you. I know you killed
Dickie. I know it was you.**

RIPLEY

Oh Marge.

He puts his hand out to control her. She pushes it away.
STARTS TO LASH OUT AT HIM, the frustration too much, so
that Ripley has to cover his face. MacCarron comes off the
boat to restrain her. Ripley looks at him as if to say: *what can
you do, she's hysterical.* MacCarron nods, pulls her on to the
boat.

MARGE

Why won't anybody listen to me!

Greenleaf catches Ripley's eye, guiltily. Turns away. They stand silhouetted as the launch revs up and surges off towards open waters, passing the little fleets of gondolas.

INT. SANTA MARIA DELLA PIETA. BRIDGE OF SIGHS. DAY.

A YOUNG BOY SINGS the soprano part of Vivaldi's *STABAT MATER*. A piercingly pure sound in Vivaldi's own church. The orchestra—rehearsing—is conducted by Peter from the organ.

Ripley slips in at the back of the church. He stands and listens. Peter sees him, smiles. Ripley smiles back.

EXT. FERRY FOR ATHENS, NAPLES. DAY.

A week later and Peter and Ripley are on the deck of the ferry, the *HELLENES*, as it sails towards Greece. They're laughing.

RIPLEY

Ask me what I want to change about this moment.

PETER

What do you want to change about this moment?

RIPLEY

Nothing.

INT. PETER'S CABIN. DUSK.

Peter's in a bathrobe organizing his currency, his traveler's checks. Ripley knocks on the door, comes in.

PETER

Hello. What are you up to?

RIPLEY
All kinds of things. Making plans.

PETER
Plans—good, plans for tonight or plans for
the future?

RIPLEY
I don't know. Both. My plan right now is to
go up on deck, look at the sunset. Come with
me.

PETER
You go. I don't want to get dressed yet.
Come back, though. Come back.
(smiles at him)
You know, you look so relaxed, like a com-
pletely different person.

RIPLEY
Well, that's entirely your fault. And, if I fall
overboard, that'll be your fault too.

EXT. DECK OF THE *HELLENES*. SUNSET.

Ripley stands on deck, staring at the magnificent sunset.
Then a voice shakes him from his reverie.

MEREDITH
Dickie? Dickie?

He turns. He's caught. Suddenly he's Dickie.

MEREDITH
Dickie, my God!

RIPLEY
Hello, Meredith.

MEREDITH
I was looking at you, your clothes, I wouldn't
have known you...

RIPLEY

Well, you've spotted me and so you get the
reward.

MEREDITH

What?

RIPLEY

Just kidding. Are you alone?

MEREDITH

Hardly. I couldn't be less alone.

Meredith points to the UPPER DECK BALCONY where TWO
OLDER COUPLES are walking around the deck.

RIPLEY

Of course. Aunt Joan.

MEREDITH

And co. A lot of co. Oh, God, I've thought
about you so much.

RIPLEY

I've thought about you.

And now he's thinking *I can't kill them all...*

MEREDITH

When I thought about you I was mostly hat-
ing you. Where've you been hiding?

RIPLEY

I haven't been hiding. I've been in police
custody. They've been trying to flush out
Freddie's killer.

MEREDITH

You're kidding.

RIPLEY

They're letting me have this vacation. Which

is why the getup. Which is why you haven't
heard from me.

MEREDITH

You know the whole world thinks you killed
Freddie? It's terrible.

RIPLEY

I know.

MEREDITH

Dickie, are you with Peter Smith-Kingsley? I
bet you are. My aunt thought she saw him.

RIPLEY

Peter Smith-Kingsley? I haven't seen him in
months. No, I'm alone.
(he understands this is not any kind of a lie)
Look, I can't talk now. Later. Later?

He kisses her. Full of future.

MEREDITH (CONT'D)

So—are you traveling under R?

RIPLEY

You know what—I am.

INT. RIPLEY'S CABIN. NIGHT.

Identical to Peter's except much more tidy. Ripley comes in.
Sits on the bed. Ripley, exhausted, on the verge of tears, covers his face with his hands.

INT. PETER'S CABIN. NIGHT.

Peter's working on his score, lying on his front, apparently
engrossed. Ripley knocks and enters. Looks long at Peter.

PETER

How was it?

RIPLEY

Good.

PETER

Was that Meredith?

RIPLEY
(sighs)

Was who Meredith?

PETER

Meredith Logue. You were kissing somebody. Looked like Meredith.

RIPLEY

Hardly kissing. Kissing off.

PETER

Didn't look that way—you know—from a distance.

RIPLEY

I lied. To her. She thought she'd seen you.

PETER

Why lie?

RIPLEY

Dickie and Peter, that's just too good gossip,
isn't it?

PETER

Or *Tom* and Peter even.

RIPLEY

Well, that would be even better gossip.

PETER

Really, why?
(completely lost)
Sorry, I'm completely lost.

RIPLEY

I know. I'm lost, too. I'm going to be stuck in

R I P L E Y (CONT'D)

the basement, aren't I, that's my, that's my—
terrible and alone and dark—and I've lied
about who I am, and where I am, and so
nobody can ever find me.

P E T E R

What do you mean *lied about who you are?*

R I P L E Y

I suppose I always thought—better to be a
fake somebody than a real nobody.

P E T E R

What are you talking about—you're not a
nobody! That's the last thing you are.

R I P L E Y

Peter, I...I...

P E T E R
(conciliatory)

And don't forget. I have the key.

R I P L E Y

You have the key. Tell me some good things
about Tom Ripley. Don't get up. Just tell me
some nice things.

He sits on the bed, leans against Peter. His eyes are brimming
with tears. He takes the cord from Peter's robe and begins
twisting it in his hands.

P E T E R

Good things about Tom Ripley? Could take
me some time! Tom is talented. Tom is
tender... Tom is beautiful...

R I P L E Y
(during this, and tender)

You're such a liar...

PETER

...Tom is musical. Tom is not a nobody.
Tom has secrets he doesn't want to tell me,
and I wish he would. Tom has nightmares.
That's not a good thing.

Ripley is pressing against him, moving up his body, kisses his
shoulder, the cord wrapped tight in his hands...

PETER (CONT'D)

Tom has someone to love him. That is a
good thing! Tom is crushing me. Tom is
crushing me!
(suddenly alarmed)
Tom, you're crushing me!

And Ripley pulls the cord tight around his neck, their struggling silhouettes filling the screen with darkness.

INT. RIPLEY'S CABIN. NIGHT.

Ripley returns to his cabin. Sits on the bed. The door of his
closet flips open with the swell and he catches his reflection.
It swings shut. Open, then shut. Through the porthole the
weather's changing as the light dies. There's a swell as the
horizon rises and falls in the round glass. Ripley, alone, in a
nightmare of his own making.

RIPLEY (O/S)

Because I didn't have a decent jacket.
Because I thought it was better to be a
fake somebody than a real nobody.

THE END.

CAIN'S MOTHER, *a lullaby*

From the silence
from the night
comes a distant lullabye

Cry, remember that first cry
Your brother standing by
and loved
both loved
beloved sons of mine
sing a lullabye
mother is close by
innocent eyes
such innocent eyes

Envy stole your brother's life
came home murdered peace of mind
left you nightmares on the pillow
sleep now

Soul, surrendering your soul
the heart of you not whole
for love
but love
what toll

Cast into the dark
branded with the mark,
of shame
of Cain

From the garden of God's light
to a wilderness of night
sleep now
sleep now.

Cast

Tom Ripley	MATT DAMON
Marge Sherwood	GWYNETH PALTROW
Dickie Greenleaf	JUDE LAW
Meredith Logue	CATE BLANCHETT
Freddie Miles	PHILIP SEYMOUR HOFFMAN
Peter Smith-Kingsley	JACK DAVENPORT
Herbert Greenleaf	JAMES REBHORN
Inspector Roverini	SERGIO RUBINI
Alvin MacCarron	PHILLIP BAKER HALL
Aunt Joan	CELIA WESTON
Colonnello Verrecchia	IVANO MARESCOTTI
Fausto	ROSARIO FIORELLO
Silvana	STEFANIA ROCCA
Fran	GRETCHEN EGOLF

Greenleaf Chauffeur	TIM MONICH
Fran's Boyfriend	FREDERICK ALEXANDER BOSCHE
Sergeant Baggio	ALESSANDRO FABRIZI
Police Officer	DARIO BERGESIO
Uncle Ted	LARRY KAPLAN
Signor Giusti	DIEGO RIBON
Gucci Assistant	CLAIRE HARDWICK
American Express Clerk	NINO PRESTER
Bus Driver	LORENZO MANCUSO
Immigration Officer	MASSIMO REALE
American Express Clerk	EMANUELE CARUCCI VITERBI
Dahlia	CATERINA DE REGIBUS
Ermelinda	SILVANA BOSI
Policeman	PIERPAOLO LOVINO
Assistant Manager	RODOLFO CORSATO
Desk Manager Aldo	GIANFRANCO BARRA
Napoli Jazz Septet	GUY BARKER (Trumpet)
	BERNARD SASSETTI (Piano)
	PERICO SAMBEAT (Alto Sax)
	GENE CALDERAZZO (Drums)
	JOSEPH LEPORE (Double Bass)
	ROSARIO GIULIANI (Tenor Sax)
	EDDY PALERMO (Electric Guitar)
San Remo Jazz Sextet	BYRON WALLEN (Cornet)
	PETE KING (Alto Sax)
	CLARKE TRACEY (Drums)
	JEAN TOUSSAINT (Tenor Sax)

	GEOFF GASCOGNE (Bass)
	CARLO NEGRONI (Piano)
Tailor	RENATO SCARPA
Silvana's Fiancé	BEPPE FIORELLO
Silvana's Brother	MARCO QUAGLIA
Photographer	MARCO ROSSI
Eugene Onegin Opera Company:	
Onegin	ROBERTO VALENTI
Lensky	FRANCESCO BOVINO
Zaretsky	STEFANO CANETTIERI
Guillot	MARCO FOTI
Silvana's mother	ALESSANDRA VANZI
Fausto's Fiancée	LUDOVICA TINGHI
Dinelli's Café Waiter	NICOLA PANNELLI
Customs Officer	PAOLO CALABRESI
Record Store Owner	PIERTO RAGUSA
Priest	ONOFRIO MANCUSO
Mr. Nichols	PAUL MOORE
Mrs. Nichols	DEBBE MOORE
Boy Singer	SIMONE EMPLER
Policemen	GIANLUCA SECCI
	MANUEL RUFFINI
San Remo Hotel Desk Clerk	ROBERTO DI PALMA
Gondolier	ENNIO MONTAGNARO
Senior American Express Official	ROBERTO CITRAN
Fletcher Longcrane	MATT McGRATH
Moose	TIM BRICKNELL
Percy	ENRICO SILVERSTRIN
American Express Official	DEIRDRE ANN HARRISON
Boat Salesman	CESARE CREMONINI

Signora Buffi	ANNA LONGHI
Grand Hotel Porter	AURELIANO AMEDEI
Stunt Coordinator	FRANCO SALAMON
Stuntmen	STEFANO MIONI
	ALESSANDRO PONTE
	CLAUDIO PACIFICO
	DAVIDE AMBROSI